Portrait of the Artist as a Young Ape

Also by Michel Butor
in English Translation

Passing Time
A Change of Heart
The Spirit of Mediterranean Places
Degrees
Mobile
Description of San Marco
Inventory
Niagara
Letters from the Antipodes
Frontiers

MICHEL BUTOR

Portrait of the Artist
as a Young Ape

a caprice

Translated from the French
by Dominic Di Bernardi

Dalkey Archive Press

Originally published as *Portrait de l'artiste en jeune singe* by Gallimard, 1967. © 1967 by Éditions Gallimard.

English translation © 1995 by Dominic Di Bernardi.

The quotations from *The Thousand and One Nights* are adapted from volume one of Richard F. Burton's translation (1885).

First Edition, 1995.

Library of Congress Cataloging-in-Publication Data
Butor, Michel.
    [Portrait de l'artiste en jeune singe. English]
    Portrait of the artist as a young ape : a caprice / Michel Butor ; translated by Dominic Di Bernardi. — 1st ed.
    p. cm.
    I. Di Bernardi, Dominic.   II. Title.
PQ2603.U73P613 1995 843'.914—dc20 94-36953
ISBN 1-56478-077-5 (cloth)
ISBN 1-56478-089-9 (paperback)

Publication of this book was made possible in part by grants from the French Ministry of Culture, the Illinois Arts Council, and the National Endowment for the Arts.

NATIONAL
ENDOWMENT
FOR ♥ THE
A R T S

Dalkey Archive Press
Illinois State University
Campus Box 4241
Normal, IL 61790-4241

Printed on permanent/durable acid-free paper and bound in the United States of America.

Contents

Prelude
Doctor H—

It was before I left for Egypt, which is to say it was quite a long time ago, because Egypt was like a second native land to me, where I lived my second childhood, so to speak.

1

The Color of Eyes

It's not often that I notice the color of someone's eyes, at least not among my acquaintances, which seems at first somewhat odd because I am very sensitive to the colors of objects—paintings, birds, flowers, clouds—and because it stands to reason that eyes would interest me more than any flower could; similarly I can be captivated by a head of hair without noticing its color.

These objects may in fact fascinate me *too* much; I'm so attracted to them that I cannot separate the color from the overall effect, especially in memory. Yes, in the middle of a crowd, among strangers, I may be struck by a certain blondness, a certain redness, seduced by a certain blackness; a country, a city, a street, or a beach may arrest my attention by the yellow of its corneas, a certain hour may be notable for the sea green of its irises. But when it comes to people I know, I have to make a deliberate effort to "see" the color of their eyes, especially the eyes.

The reason is that I can look at a person's hands, feet, or forehead without being in his gaze, but if I focus on the eyes, I'm not simply looking at the eyes but at him: I look at him through his eyes.

The eye blinds me to itself, and I fully understand why the ancients often compared the eye to the sun.

Only when I fail to look at someone properly, only when I don't see him as a person, does his eye become a glass eye, one object among others, not the source illuminating the person's depths, leading me to his secret.

Consequently, it doesn't surprise me at all that the color of eyes is one of the most important parts of the description on identification papers; a policeman's scrutiny, his way of studying a face, is exactly what allows him to isolate the color of an eye. But using this manner of perception to describe people in everyday conversation perturbs me. Some people seem to disengage themselves at the earliest opportunity from that haunting, questioning little pupil by blocking it out behind the tint that surrounds it, which one has noted and captured once and for all. They take cover behind that thin film, find refuge behind that ready-made means of identity; they know right away how to "identify" that other, that intruder, if something ever goes wrong, if something new and incriminating suddenly arises in their way of seeing things.

But for the person who knows and wants to look into the eyes, the color of the iris will always be a problem, a danger zone, because someone will ask him the color of his lover's eyes, and that person will be surprised that he has never "noticed," which will lead to another surprise: really, am I as fascinated as that?

This color becomes his quest: he begins by overcoming somehow his usual way of seeing things, plunges into the waters of this gaze to go and pluck that flower from the islands of that other shore, closes his own in order to bring it back to his own island, there to display it in his public square or on his quay, so that he can study it in the absence of the other.

Here we should praise the old masters of portrait-painting. Surely no one would dream of accusing them of having neglected their models, of failing to look "into their eyes." It is obvious that if they had contented themselves with applying the "identifying" color to the iris on the canvas, that which had been noted and used in conversation, their painting would not have had the least bit of life, because of all the face's features the eye is the only one that can't be painted "from nature," especially with that intense expressivity that the greatest succeed in giving to it, in guarding intact.

For after a quarter of an hour of posing, no model could continue to look at an artist in such a way, and it was only after the eye was averted that the artist took up the task of rediscovering it alive on the canvas.

First, he had to lose the color of the eyes, to blur it into the background of his focus, before he could reconstruct it, to use it to create the necessary liaison between the black of the pupil and all the easily verifiable coloration of the cheeks, cheekbones, eyebrows, even the eyelids, the only kind of liaison that permits us to "dwell" in that black double point in the same way one dwelled in the stare of that man during its moments of greatest intensity, which is to say, during those moments when it was impossible to pay attention to the color of the eyes.

It is from the other side of those eyes into which he so passionately plunged (lovingly, malevolently, devotedly, curiously) that he rediscovered it emerging in his work, like an alchemist bent over his athanor, surprised at its appearance, completely new, the unique solution to an equation whose terms consisted of his complete knowledge of humanity and what he had already painted.

I knew Doctor H— too well to be able to tell the color of his eyes; I had not studied him enough to be able to paint them.

2
Hungarian

He had a high forehead. I'm tempted to say that his hair
was graying, but upon reflection, I don't think that was
the case; perhaps I saw it graying later, or maybe only
now that he is dead I imagine him older than he actually
was. He couldn't have been more than forty at the time.
A Hungarian

(that puddle of Asia left behind after the waves of in-
vasions behind the dike of the distant Carpathians, a
rugged mass for me, all those forests and gorges, the
castles full of machinery and obsessions as in a Jules
Verne novel, with legends of vampires, O Nosferatu!

—especially that language, so different from ours,
those faces with high cheekbones; did he have high
cheekbones?

—there was a tradition on my mother's side of the family concerning a certain Ergatus Toxer, one of Atilla's
lieutenants, who founded a dynasty in the region of the
Catalaunian fields, to whom one traced, by way of
onomastic similarities, certain ancestors from Châlon,
always a source of amusement among my brothers, even
if I did believe, in my rages or in my dreams, that I had a
little bit of the Hun in me,

—I never said anything to him, but he asked me, as
did many others afterward, if I were Hungarian, because

my name (which, originating elsewhere, has nothing to do with their history) can be seen everywhere on the streets of Budapest, where *butor* means *furniture,*

—the immensity of that plain, which I had traversed while in my seat via a documentary, *Horses of the Puszta,* seen at the Cinémathèque Française, in which one witnesses in particular the birth of a mare (that enormous bubble from which the colt broke free with difficulty, the trembling legs on which it tried to stand),

—the prestige of the twin city of Budapest with its enormous Danube, the parliamentary palace, whose outline in another time adorned postage stamps, the crown of the king Saint Stephen, the czardas in the restaurants,

—the music, naturally, Franz (Férenc) Liszt, Béla Bartók, the rhapsodies,

—the Tokay wine, which I had not yet sampled but which I dreamed of tasting one day, an elixir according to the enthusiastic reports of Alexandre Dumas . . .)

refugee, he was required, in order to practice medicine in France, to present a new thesis, on Paracelsus, on whom he was a leading authority. He lived in a small apartment on rue du Val-de-Grâce, in the same building that today houses the consulate of the People's Republic of Hungary, crammed with books on alchemy, English ghost stories, and science fiction novels. He loaned them to me readily, and allowed me to study the most amazing drawings.

3

Days of Reading

Before and during the war, I spent my holidays, along with my six brothers and sisters and six cousins, in a village in the French Vexin, where our grandmother maintained a house, two in fact: the second, on the other side of a lane, sheltered in one of its rooms a ponderous piece of old sacristy furniture full of books. There was also a library in the main house, but only books deemed "suitable" (for adults or children) were kept there. The old, unsuitable books, ancient and often quite beautiful editions of Montesquieu and Rousseau, were relegated to the other side.

Once a year we were invited to dust them. We donned huge aprons, armed ourselves with dust rags, pulled down all the books and all the "unusable" objects (just as the books were "unsuitable," the objects were unusable but fascinating nonetheless: a shark's jawbone, a hussar's epaulets, old pastry molds, ancient retorts made of very thick glass . . .), replaced the old newspapers on the shelves with new, wiped everything clean, and put everything back in order.

Wonderful times in the swirling dust, the rustle of pages and bindings.

A notebook bound in foxed and wrinkled parchment (we wondered whether it were made of human skin)

15

exerted a special fascination; I have it still.

On the back cover, on rough cardboard, written in a large hand, one could read:

This book belongs to Father Azothini. 1729.

Inside on the flyleaf, in a completely different handwriting—fine, distinguished, ornate, with flourishes at the ends of certain words and the crossbars of the *t*s quite low, so long and straight they seemed to be crossouts at first:

This curious production made quite a stir in its tyme and today remains keenly sought after by those lunaticks who are trying to discover the Philosopher's Stone; they cannot yet procure it for its weight in silver.

The title page reads:

THE NATURAL PHILOSOPHY
OF THREE RENOUNED ANCIENT PHILOSOPHERS
ARTEPHIUS, FLAMEL, & SYNESIUS
Concerning the occult arts and the transmutation of metals.

Latest edition, augmented with a short
Treatise on Mercury, and on the Philosopher's Stone
by G. Ripleus, newly translated into the French language.
PARIS, from the house of LAURENT d'HOURY,
on the Quay des Augustins, by the statue of Saint John.
MDCLXXXII
By consent of His Royal Majesty

According to Ripley's treatise and the copyright page, it is an unabridged reprint of an edition from 1612, "at the expense of the Distinguished Translator," Pierre Arnauld, seigneur of the knighthood, gentleman of Poitiers.

How I loved his language and his sly urbanity:

Oure Artephivs (beneuolent reader), alone among all other Philosophers, is never envyous, thus as he himself sayeth afterward in many places, this is the reason for which he explains in his Treatise the whole of the art in plain and simple language, interpreting as much as he may the ambages and sophismes of others. Still in order that the impivs, ignorant and the wicked may not easily discouer the means to harm the good by learning this Science, he has slightly veiled the principles of the art, by an artful method . . .

What a delightful quiver was introduced into my reading by, among other things, the uncertainty between *u*
and *v!*

> . . . Therefor read this volum, indeed reread it, until you have it
> by heart and can obtain the ends desird. It would be superfluous to
> speak more of our avthor, it is enough that he liveth the length of a
> thousand years, by the grace of God and the use (as he avers) of
> that quintessence. That itself is testified to by Roger Bacon in his
> volum of admirable works of Nature; and again by the very
> learned Theophrastus Paracelsus in his volum on long life, which
> time of one thousand years no other Philosopher, not even Father
> Hermes, has been able to attain. So look upon these pages then,
> and consider whether (perhaps) this avthor has not more thor-
> oughly than others understood how to use this stone. Whatever
> the case, such as it is, use it, and may our labors be to the glory of
> God and the usefulness of the Kingdom of France. God be with
> you.

Artephius' text is given in facing Latin and French
pages, Flamel's in French alone, due to the material limi-
tations of the book which Pierre Arnaud sets forth for us
in his salutation

(I wish I could reproduce here the beautiful ornate initial):

> I would have liked (dear Reader) to provide those commentaries
> also in Latin and French which I have made on Artephivs, but
> due to the various illustrations that need oft be depicted I have
> been able to proffer them to you in one language alone . . .

(charming, those wood engravings in pure Gothic
style, in all likelihood reprinted from an earlier Latin
text edition:

the two dragons,

man and woman.

The figure of a man resembling Saint Paul bearing an
unsheathed glaive, a man kneeling at his feet . . .),

for patriotic reasons also:

> . . . However, I have chosen the French version so that first of
> all good Frenchmen can freely understand the words, and thus
> have no need to run to foreign nations whose curiosity about them
> is great compared to that of France . . .

Ink illustrations alone:

Three people raised from the dead, two men and one woman, two angels above, and on the angels, the figure of the savior coming to judge the world,

but whose full colors were indicated by their captions at the head of each chapter:

On a violet and blue field, two orange Angels and their scrolls,

their descriptions within the text:

On the left hand side is Saint Peter with his key, garbed in citrine red, resting his hand on a woman wearing an orange robe . . .

and especially their interpretations according to the magisterium of Hermes.

In the last illustration, look at the flaming clothing of the man who is holding a winged lion by the paws as though abducting it:

Praise be God eternally, who has granted us the grace to see his beautiful and absolutely perfect purpurin color, this beautiful color of Pauot Syluestre of Rocher, this shimmering, flaming Tyrrhenian color, impervious to change or alteration, on which Heaven itself, and its Zodiac can no longer hold dominion or power, whose beaming, blinding brilliance seems almost to impart to man a supercelestial quality, making him (when he studies and learns to know it) grow astonished, tremble and quiver all at once.

And how I could only dream of those other illustrations that were merely mentioned, heart of that other book:

Therefore I, NICOLAS FLAMEL, writer, whoso after the death of my parents earned my living in our Art of Writing, establishing inventories, drawing up accounts, and producing statements of expense for tutors and their charges, there fell into my hands for the sum of two florins, a very old and extremely large gilt-edged book . . .

about this superbook:

. . . it was neither in paper nor parchment, like other books, but made only of supple bark (such was my impression) of tender shrubs. It had a very supple leather cover, completely inscribed with letters or strange illustrations, and in my opinion I believe they might well have been Greek characters or some other such ancient language. So many were there I was unable to read and I am quite sure they were neither notes, nor Latin or Gallic letters, because we have some understanding of those. As for the contents, its bark leaves were inscribed, and showed a very high degree of craftsmanship, written with an iron stylus in beautiful and very clear colored Latin letters . . .

a myth which permeates all alchemical literature (as it does, more or less traceably, literature as a whole), which would truly be the stone and the path, of which all known books are merely pale reflections:

. . . On the first leaf there was written in large gilt capitals: ABRAHAM THE JEW, PRINCE, LEVITE PRIEST, ASTROLOGER, AND PHILOSOPHER, TO THE JEWISH PEOPLE THROUGH GOD'S READING, DISPERSED AMONG THE GAULS, GREETINGS. D.I. After that it was full of great curses and maledictions (with this word, MARANATHA, which was often repeated there), against any person who might glance upon this book without being a High Priest or Scribe.

The book has seen much use, because it is smudged in many places. There are signs in the margins: arrows, triangles, stars, dashes, crosses. Certain passages are underlined, for instance in Artephius:

the impure is stationary earth,

very lovingly she with the other conjoined,

The body composed of male and female, of Sun and Moon;

O followers, if any still exist, may these minimal instructions lighten your labors!

And the fact that he was Hungarian allowed me to identify Doctor H— even more closely with one of the characters in the alchemical theater, the one who appears at the end of the famous treatise, *About the Great Stone of the Ancient Sages of Brother Basile Valentin of the Order of Saint Benoit,* since translated into French by Eugène Canseliet and published by Editions de Minuit:

There was seen approaching a very elderly man with hair and beard white as snow, clothed in purple from head to toe . . . And as, that instant, all stood quiet, he began in this manner:

"Wake up, man, and contemplate the light, do not allow the shadows to seduce you! The Gods of fortune and the higher Gods have instructed me through a deep sleep. O how happy is he who recognizes the Gods, what astonishing wonders they perform! Happy is he whose eyes are open, so that he can see the light which has been hidden from him! . . .

"Hungary first begot me; the sky and the stars maintain me and even the earth suckles me. Forced to die and be buried, I am nevertheless reborn through Vulcan. It is because Hungary is my fatherland and my mother encompasses the world . . ."

4

Turba Philosophorum

During the Occupation, I took a course at the Louis-le-Grand lycée taught by Monsieur C—, author of a widely read handbook of philosophy, and one of my uncles, an old man with a long white beard stained brown by tobacco juice, to whom we, the whole family together, regularly wished a happy new year during the first week of January

(of the small living room into which we were led, we saw the desk through the half-opened door, the book-lined walls, and an enormous table that occupied almost the entire room, covered with papers, filled with clouds of cold smoke),

former professor at the Polytechnique and later at the Collège de France, a Bergsonian, one of the leading figures in the Modernism controversy and a close friend of Teilhard de Chardin,

and who held, at the Sorbonne, a series of lectures on the problem of God, which I must admit had never ceased to vex me: an excellent occasion for my own instruction.

A certain number of young Thomists showed up to cause a ruckus

(yes, one might have the impression these discussions took place centuries ago);

heart pounding, I joined in on the subsequent controversies, straining to catch every word, occasionally venturing a remark, with the result that I became acquainted with the woman who had organized the conference and who invited me to participate in some colloquies that were to be held in the environs of Paris at a castle famous for its Flaubertian associations.

We met in front of the Balzar bar, in the rue des Ecoles. We were to leave on a bus. She managed to find buses at a time when only bicycles rode through the streets, when a passing truck, even a German one, was an event. I didn't dare relax over a drink while waiting. I paced the sidewalk, discreetly greeting the people that I knew. We boarded the bus. We took off. Bouncing. Suburbs. People struck up conversations.

This went on for several years, both before and after the Liberation. I can no longer distinguish between the different sessions, nor when I saw this person or that.

At first there were other students, others from lycées or like myself, also writers, doctors, theologians of every stripe, and especially professors of all ages representing a variety of disciplines.

Many of them are famous today, others completely forgotten, even by me. Some I mix up, confusing their names, faces, their denominations; their first names or titles may have traded places. I drank in their words.

I felt as though I had discovered a password, an Open Sesame, a secret entrance, allowing me to enter, almost on false pretenses, a cavern of intellectual treasures, of discussions that deserved to be copied down in golden ink on leaves of purple, or better yet engraved, with the utmost skill, using an iron stylus, in beautiful and very clear colored Latin letters, on the supple bark of tender saplings, the open entrance to the palace closed to the king himself.

Ah, to be sure, I did not find that everything that reached my ears was of the same quality, and I clearly recognized the ignorance and callousness of some of the eminent dignitaries in that domain which so captivated me, but they nonetheless were, for me, "their magnificences," despite their shabby apparel, their underfed physiques, their worries, their war-weary faces—grand dignitaries of a court without a caliph, of a famous academy of Baghdad or Laputa.

I followed them at some distance during their walks, respectful, ears pricked, vigilant. There were only a few I dared to approach, to whom I dared occasionally to address a remark, a novice in a floating monastery. The very air, agitated by their learned talk or even by their most ordinary civilities, seemed charged with formulas and keys, which I struggled to collect and compare.

It was spring, a time of deprivation, the Age of Lead; it was very cold for the most part. The castle was sparsely furnished: in each room a cot with a straw mattress and army blankets, a folding garden chair. The warden's house was heated, providing a modicum of comfort for older couples. We met for a lunch no more frugal than that to which I had become accustomed for the past few years, and the surrounding lawns were transformed into superb meadows, the grass as tall as I was, with several paths cut by a scythe, as though by explorers through a wild savanna.

It was an era of lofty discourse and learned questions, of leisurely approaches and of meditation. It was knowledge in all its splendor, inquiry in all the depth of its perplexities, freed at last from all the tattered trappings of the classroom. There the professors were accessible; it was a training ground for boldness, full of fresh breezes and gentle austerity, a Thélème of poverty, amidst magnificent trees, with the war whispering in the background, the reign of Saturn changed into a golden century.

And all those who were there, even the youngest, by virtue of the simple fact they were there, by the fact they had been chosen to board that bus that seemed like such an ordinary bus (even though in those days to see in the streets of Paris a plain bus that wasn't a military bus, and later a nonmilitary French or Allied one, was indeed an extraordinary sight), this bus of which none of my friends from Louis-le-Grand, or later from the Sorbonne, if they had passed by at that moment, could imagine what was inside, to what it served as the antichamber, one and all, by the fact that they entered the cold, upon beds such as those, each and every one of them, despite the barbarity, the crudeness or the pretension they were capable of displaying in certain respects, could become, in at least one sphere—"masters."

In the midst of this scene, there was only myself, who was nothing, who knew nothing, who could teach nothing to anyone whomsoever, who enjoyed a distinguished favor which, to be sure, I didn't intend to let slip through my fingers, myself, and perhaps a handful of others my age, but, as far as they were concerned, I wasn't at all certain; they struck me as so eloquent; they were masters at least of a fluid ease, a quick-tongued responsiveness. In their eyes, through their youth, I was able to read years, years, an entire lifetime of studies, of solitude and of complicity with other bright young-old men, other young hermits in the middle of the city, in the middle of secondary school, right in the middle of the Ecole Normale Supérieure, in the heart of the Sorbonne as well, but in other courses, other young virtuosos, prodigies, graduates of one program or another, the cause of wonder, of hope, almost of jealousy in their professors.

They spoke, laughed, and I mingled with them; it was understandable, from the point of view of the others, that theirs was the group I was supposed to belong to, and they accepted me, tolerated me; to be sure, I wasn't one of them, but I didn't bother them; and often I didn't understand the reason for their laughter, and often their conversation was quite obscure to me, and certain of their words plunged me into hours of thought and puzzlement.

I was a lay brother, I was an ape.

That was where I met Doctor H—, master of ghosts.

5

The Invitation

One day, a few years later (I had come by to return Algernon Blackwood, H. P. Lovecraft, or the Président d'Espagnet), Doctor H— asks me whether I want to spend a few weeks of my school vacation in Germany, in one of the most beautiful castles he had ever seen.

He shows me some postcards, old sepia prints that looked as though they were from the last century, towers, a jagged silhouette . . .

He had just spent some time in Franconia, at the home of his old friend Alexandre von B—, poet, storyteller, who long ago in Vienna had been a close friend of Hofmannsthal and his whole circle, but also a leading practitioner of spagyric medicine, preparing in his dispensary, according to the ancient recipes, those of Paracelsus in particular, electuaries, balms, salves, and tinctures which he sent to numerous correspondents under the Sol-Luna Laboratory label.

There he had met a certain Count W—, who had been forced from his estate in the Sudetenland when Bavaria was transformed into a people's democracy, and sought refuge in the vicinity, in the very town in question, boasting a museum and especially an enormous library, property of Prince von O— W—, his uncle through marriage, for whom he acted as curator.

Count W— was seeking a young Frenchman to help re-acquaint himself with the French language. I simply needed to write him.

I'd already been to Germany, first as part of a group of military trainees (it was mandatory in those days), of which my first brother-in-law was one of the officers, in the Saar, in a boarding school that had emptied out for the holidays, at the top of a hill. We were in uniform, and I had the hardest time, before each inspection, in giving my hideous forage cap a tolerable tilt.

After that, I had participated in international student meetings, in a luxurious inn built a few years earlier for the S.A. in the Black Forest on the banks of the Titisee. The agenda at that time was to fraternize, to denazify; study groups and songs.

That was how I became acquainted with large earthen-ware ovens, wooden seats under double windows, white wine dyed blue for the holidays, vomit tanks whose handles were affixed to the tiled walls of latrines,

and long cross-country ski treks through the woods, ending in the evening with a trip across the frozen lake to regain shelter.

One summer day, near another inn where we'd come to receive the visit of Martin Heidegger

(since this was the only time I ever saw him, I have a perfect memory of his blue eyes; it seemed to me he was wearing a forester's outfit),

a large, sloping meadow, very stony, which was stream-ing, murmuring magnificently with water; plus a strong wind, and very high on the horizon, racing clouds;

another German philosopher who participated in our discussions and outings, climbing alongside me, whis-pered in my ear:

"Do you remember that passage where Jacob Böhme speaks of the flowing streams of the soul?"

(Doctor H— naturally owned the collected works of Jacob Böhme.)

That was how I'd learned a little German and a little bit about Germany. The land, language of philosophers. And I sensed my way through the verses of early poets, the pages of modern authors, as in the books of alchemy. Ah, how the obscure streams of the German language flowed for me! To make some progress, to steep myself in it more completely—wouldn't these have been reasons enough to have me enthusiastically accept the doctor's proposal? I wrote, I received a letter from the count, I was welcome to come, I left.

Alas, German language, how I've lost you since then!

Journey

The Holy Empire

In Egypt, the god of writing, Thoth, was often portrayed as an ape.

1
Going There

A few days before I left, maybe the day before, I received a phone call from Doctor H— asking me to drop everything and come by his place immediately.

I rush over to rue du Val-de-Grâce. He opens the door.

"Listen: I have something I need you to do. Would you please deliver this as soon as possible to Alexander von B—? He knows about your trip. He's expecting you."

It was a package approximately ten inches by six, two inches thick, wrapped in brown paper, tied with a white string. Just by feeling it you could tell it held leaves of paper. Perhaps it was a book, an old tattered book.

"Is it a book?"

"Yes, it's a book."

Followed by a sardonic smile.

I think that I dared to sneak a look only after my train was rolling across Germany at night, my fingers shaking as I undid the knot, tore the wrapping. It was a copy of *The Philosophic Abodes* by Fulcanelli, which left me somewhat disappointed, for I had already read this book over which André Breton had just waxed enthusiastic.

At the time copies were hard to come by. Since then it's been reprinted. I must surely have reread a few passages before redoing the package.

I had another book in my suitcase: the French translation of *Joseph in Egypt* by Thomas Mann.

In the morning I could make out the dark profile of the Ulm cathedral.

The black and white lettering of the German train stations.

The trains were still moving very slowly.

I had to change at Augsburg.

I was certainly still half asleep, unwashed, unshaven, disheveled, my eyes and hair gritty from the train smoke. I must have been hungry. I was almost there.

I made out the name of my destination. Count W— had written that he would meet me. Nobody. The letter was in German. Had I got it wrong? I step off the train. No one; just a woman behind the gate. I muster up my vocabulary and ask her the way to the castle.

"Are you Monsieur Butor?"

"Yes."

"The count has asked me to apologize for him because he was unable to come for you."

"Is he away?"

"No, no, he's here."

"Is he ill?"

"No, not ill, he has a . . ."

It was a word which I'd never come across in my scholarly readings.

"He has a what?"

"He can't walk."

"Did he break a leg?"

"Oh no, don't worry. Do you want to come with me? Give me your suitcase."

"I can carry it just fine, I assure you."

"So then your trip hasn't been too tiring?"

The words failed me. I couldn't see anymore. I did my best to smile, while sighing. She also did her best to smile, but she looked perturbed. She must have felt a little sorry for me. She launched into an explanation which I couldn't follow at all. In desperation we started

on our way. To our right and left there were trees, there
was the path. It climbed, I followed her, I couldn't man-
age to keep up, she slowed down, stopped, turned around
toward me, I had paused to catch my breath, I quickened
my pace a little, I came up alongside her, stopped, set
down my suitcase, smiled at her, panted, we started off
again, I switched hands with my suitcase, there were
houses, trees, dust, I was sweating, thirsty, hungry,
what time could it be, the afternoon was already gone,
the path kept climbing . . .

Then I let her take my suitcase; it was better that way,
we walked much faster that way, I even had trouble
keeping up with her that way, she slowed down, smiled,
spoke to me, she could see that I didn't understand her;
but just a moment ago I was able to, and I was speaking
to her . . .

Trees, path, a panoramic view, the path, a door, sunshine, dust, the path, ramparts, another door, an
enormous courtyard full of grass, towers, a small door in
a tower, stairs, a landing, another door, a vestibule, a
large room with three windows looking out on a courtyard; she sets down her suitcase and disappears behind
me.

In the center, seated in an armchair, one leg propped
across a stool, his foot bandaged, cane within reach, a
man dressed in gray, sitting very upright, short hair,
was playing solitaire. Behind him, on the wall, above a
sofa, a large life-size frontal portrait of a young man
standing who looked like him, in a German army officer's
uniform with the iron cross.

"Monsieur Butor? Take off your coat. I have the
impression that you felt warm during your trip. Did everything go well? I've had a slight sprain, but it'll be better tomorrow. Here's the sofa where you'll be sleeping.
This is the portrait of my brother who died during the
Russian campaign . . ."

His wife, his children: a boy and a girl, dinner; there

was nothing to drink on the table; after the meal, a glass of beer was brought to the count and to me.

Nighttime.

Above my bed the rustic baroque ceiling unfurled its soft pink arabesques and its stucco cherubs.

I dreamed rather actively during my stay; but if the events of the previous day can always sooner or later be verified, even those thought to be the most secret, by some researcher, thanks to a thousand and one ruses, a thousand and one detours and games of patience,

—in the same way some future sleuth might be able to pick out the errors, oversights, distortions in these few pages!—

by contrast, for the moment there is no way of certifying that a man has indeed dreamed on a certain night what he tells us that he has dreamed, if he hasn't noted it down the next day right after waking,

no way of detecting a lie or an error in the story of a dream;

so, rather than claim to remember any dreams I may have had at the castle of H—, remember well enough to be able to note them down after so many years, I prefer to deliberately reconstruct them,

dreaming methodically about those long-lost vanished dreams.

2
𝒯𝒽ε 𝒱ε𝓇𝓎 𝐸𝓁𝒹ε𝓇𝓁𝓎 𝒜ℓ𝒶𝓃

I was barely out of high school; the professor, my mentor with the yellowish eye, noticing in me much curiosity, called upon all those who excelled in the sciences and the fine arts to come and cultivate it.

I memorized the entire **Mysterium Magnum,** *that wonderful book in which glimmered the roots, the precepts, and the rules of our sect; in order to gain a more thorough knowledge, I read the works of the most approved authors who had clarified it with their commentaries.*

Anxious to discover everything possible concerning our cult, I set about a special investigation of our legends, increasing my knowledge about emblems, the way our musicians sight-read in the art of the fugue; I devoted particular attention to the description of imaginary lands and fabled epochs, and in composing a sort of underside to our language, without nevertheless neglecting the least of the exercises recommended to students.

But what I liked very much, my chief success, was engraving with an iron stylus upon supple bark the characters of our German writing. I made so much progress that I surpassed the calligraphers who had achieved the highest reputations.

The public carried the news of my talents all the way to the University of the Holy Empire, whose illustrious blue-eyed rector, curious to see me, sent to my delighted professor an assistant assigned to shower him with praise and extend me an invitation.

I took a week-long trip with this man on a bus especially chartered because of the length and difficulty of the road; under a cloud of dust, several armored trucks surrounded us.

Unable to resist their weapons, we declared ourselves to be delegates of the great rector, hoping thus to save our library and our lives, but the soldiers answered us insolently:

"Why would you like us to respect your teacher? We aren't even on his academy's land . . ."

They attacked, pillaged, relentlessly.

Alone, injured, deprived of any hope for rescue in a strange land, I didn't dare continue along the main highway for fear of falling back into their hands. I walked across an immense wild savanna, whose grass was as tall as I was, a puddle of Asia, at the foot of a very high mountain, with jagged peaks, amid its forests and gorges, castles with machinery and obsessions, midway along which, in grottoes, flowed several beautiful fountains where herds of horses moving down from the highlands in various spots came to drink.

I passed the night rather timorously after having eaten some roots that I had dug up along the way.

A week later, I walked into a large, very populous city, watered by a large blue river, where music perpetually filled the air. The rhapsodies, the dances, the quartets that reached my ears muffled for a few moments the sadness I felt at seeing myself in such a state: my face, my hands, my feet blackened, encrusted with dirt, my shoes worn, my clothes in tatters, and my cheekbones now protruding.

As I was deciphering, amid the strange inscriptions

(and as for myself, I believed that I might well be dealing with Egyptian words or some other such ancient language),

engraved countless times on supple bark (so it seemed to me) from tender shrubs, the word furniture *in beautiful and very clear colored Latin letters, I could see coming toward me a very elderly man with black eyes, beard and hair white as snow, dressed in purple from head to toe, holding in his hand a caduceus, two snakes entwined, the emblem of medicine, who addressed me, much to my surprise, in refined French, asking who I was, where I was coming from, and what had brought me there.*

I concealed nothing of what had happened to me, but when I had finished speaking, instead of offering me consolation, he added to my miseries:

"Greatly beware," he said, "of confiding to anyone what you have just told me; for the rector of this university is the greatest enemy of your own professor and mentor, and he would no doubt dishonor you in some way if he were to learn that you've arrived in this city."

I thanked him for the advice he gave, and indicated that his sound counsel would be my sole guide.

Since he deemed that I had need of something to restore me, he ordered for me a glass of Tokay, and even offered me a cot in his consulting room, which I accepted.

A week later, noticing that I had sufficiently recovered from the fatigue of my long, arduous trip, and aware that the majority of the students of our sect, in order to have something to fall back on during hard times, learned one or another sort of art or craft, he asked me, with orange eyes, if I knew any which might allow me to live without being a burden to anyone.

I answered that I knew major and minor logic, that I was a contrapuntist, mytholographer, and most of all, that I knew how to write perfectly the characters of German writing.

"With all that you've just told me," he replied, "you won't earn enough to buy a crust of bread in this country; nothing here is more useless than that sort of knowledge. If you want to follow my advice," he went on, with azure

eyes, "you'll don the outfit of an apprentice assistant forester, and, even though you strike me as a clumsy weakling, you'll enter the nearby Black Forest and peel off the barks of tender shrubs, set them out for sale on Parliament Square, and I assure you that you'll bring in enough to allow you to earn your keep without relying on anyone whomsoever. By such means you'll enable yourself to bide your time until heaven dissipates the cloud of ill fortune which is crossing the happiness of your life, forcing you to hide your scholarly expertise; I'll take care of finding you a cover and a stylus."

The very next day, the very elderly man, my host, brought me a yellowish costume with blue belt and black boots, orange buttons engraved with two azure dragons, with a copper cover and an iron stylus, and recommending me to a group of poor Jews, dispersed throughout the Kingdom of Hungary and who earned their living in the same way, he requested, his eyes moon blue, that they take me with them.

They led me into the forest of the Carpathians, and each day I brought back in my completely engraven cover three times seven leaves, which I sold for a half-florin each; for, although this black mountain was not far off, the bark nonetheless sold at a very high price in this city, due to the few people who took the trouble to go and peel it.

A week later, I returned to the elderly man with eyes citrine-silver white as his hair and beard, the sum he had lent me.

Alone, and having entered a gorge further than usual, coming to a very pleasant spot, I was watching glimmer, in the hollow of an oak, a silver ring attached to a moonstone trap completely engraven with strange letters or figures

(and in my opinion, I believed that they might well be Egyptian hieroglyphics or some other such ancient writing), *covered with snow which I removed.*

After lifting it, I could see steps going down under the earth; I went down with my stylus.

The sumptuous underground abode echoed with a din that excited my great admiration, as though it were located at the most bustling spot on the earth's surface . . .

3
The Library

At breakfast the next day, Tuesday, the count's leg was still causing him pain; he apologized for not being able to accompany me; he hoped that by the afternoon he could begin my tour of the castle, but for now, it doubtless would be best if I wandered around in the village streets below.

I thanked him for his suggestions, helped him into a large armchair near the round table in the room where my bed had just been made, exactly as on the day before when I arrived, brought him a footstool, and left him just as he began a game of solitaire called Almanach de Gotha, the rules of which he was to explain to me a few days later:

dealing the cards three at a time from the deck held in his hand, always turning the third one face up, reshuffling the deck when picking up the cards to start over

(this procedure was the same for all the varieties of solitaire I was already familiar with, as well as those he would teach me during my visit),

he then married off the kings with the queens, always of different suits, and placed them in a row,

these couples engendered jacks, or princes, all of the same suit as the king their father, placed in a second row, which he had to marry to tens, or princesses, always of a different suit,

who gave birth to the nines (dukes); and so the game progressed, with the sevens (counts), the fives (marquises), the threes (knights), until you reached the aces, commoners who could find no wives.

Then I went back down, in a much better mood, hands in pockets, whistling a tune while going over German verb conjugations, by the same route that I had climbed with such difficulty the day before.

After cutting a wide arc across a gentle slope through the orchards, I set foot on the streets of the village, where I wandered nonchalantly

—most of them too narrow for car traffic—

zigzagging from shop window to shop window, often at the risk of stumbling against one old man or another in buckskins, admiring the large paving stones, the exposed beams of the old houses, the signs in front of the shops, the barber's shaving basin, a beautifully baroque pharmacy, the pointed roofs, the river W— where swans and white ducks swam, the bridge and the windmill in its ornate gable,

listening to the conversations of the passersby, of which I couldn't catch a single word, not even the "Grüss Gott" (God bless you) repeated so often, which I had never heard before in the Saarland or in the Black Forest,

and mostly sharpening my skills by deciphering signs, placards, and inscriptions

—because I had never succeeded in accustoming myself to German orthography—

delighted when I could translate them: The Sunlit Pub, Hotel Swann, Furniture, which didn't happen very often.

In the afternoon, the count—walking very slowly, leaning on his cane, greeting everyone he encountered with a sonorous "Grüss Gott"—took me to see the first wall,

which encircled a small village higher up the mountain, partly in ruins though still inhabited by several elderly people, with a double portal, small hidden doors
leading to the paths that descended directly toward the
cluster below, a balcony overlooking the roofs, the former
stables, restaurants, butcher shop, the former keep
where coin was minted, the granges, the tiny gardens.

Passing between the white tower and the red stable,
built against the prison tower, we climbed to the upper
wall.

"Turn around," the count told me. "There, above the
portcullis, is the head of the last wolf killed in the region."

"When?"

"I don't know exactly, before my arrival at any rate;
you must ask in the village. You will have all the time
you need to admire the parapet walk, one of the best preserved of its kind. I think it's time you have a first look at
the second largest private library in Germany, 140,000
volumes, most of which are from eighteenth-century
France. Only major authors are missing, because the
first editions of Diderot, Rousseau, Voltaire, and certain
highly sought illustrated books were sold at the turn of
the century to pay estate duties. They have just finished
relocating the library here in this enormous Renaissance
building. It had been scattered among the prince's seven
castles before now."

He spoke a refined, fluent, old-fashioned French, quite
exquisite, with a certain hardness to his consonants and
the singsong cadence of southern Germany,
   stumbling only now and then over a noun's gender, or
asking me for a word that had slipped his memory.

At the entrance hung an old, inferior painting of Charlemagne.

There was an entire room of incunabula,
   a treasure house where one could admire an illumi-
nated Irish manuscript from the seventh century, and an

ivory Romanesque crucifix, smaller but no less beautiful than the one in the Bamberg cathedral,

a collection of somber-colored tapestries from Franconia,

stained-glass windows placed in a corner turret from whose large windows one could view the outside world (it was almost the only spot along the enormous wall where such a thing was possible, except for the loopholes and breaches of the parapet walk), and in one of them the count drew my attention to the emerald green glass used to represent the wood of the cross, for that color was particularly difficult to obtain and thus was reserved for only the most sacred objects,

a shelf of books on alchemy; picking up the *Musæum Hermeticum* and paging through Maier's Latin, I found:

The moon also finally appeared and, in front of her, Dialectic spread a resplendent veil of silver, on which Prudence was depicted clothed in a celestial hue . . .

a painting by Bernhard Strigel, wood sculptures by Tilman Riemenschneider and Veit Stoss,

a shelf of theosophical works—taking up the *Mysterium Magnum,* with difficulty I was able to decipher the Old German:

We name the second day Moon for the reason that the Moon rules the first hour . . .

at least five storeys, with a large rotunda at the very top, where sitting in rows was the complete collection of the *Cabinet des Fées* and the *Imaginary Voyages,* the novels of Crébillon fils, *The Adventures of Faublas,* around a small oval table where there was left lying

(to be sure, it was the only book left lying about in the whole building)

a small, badly damaged volume:

. . . I descended the steps to the bottom and came to a door, which I opened, and found myself in a noble hall strong of structure and beautifully built, where was a damsel like a pearl of great price, whose favor banished from my heart all grief and cark and care . . .

"It really looks like you've never read them. You'll have a great deal of time, my dear boy, seven weeks!"

Daylight was waning. I blushed. His leg was clearly hurting him very much now, and we still had all the stairs to go down. But he insisted on showing me everything on this last floor: the newspaper room, the room for popular novels, for English periodicals, and, in the turret, various family mementos, in particular the uniform of an officer who died in 1870.

The view from the windows looked down upon a round hill with a few trees, with just the qualities a Flemish painter of the fifteenth century would look for in a model for a rising landscape.

Wall-dwelling falcons with nests under the rafters were circling, shrieking.

I walked down much faster than the count. I heard his cane tapping on each step. I wanted to see if I'd be able to find that page in Jacob Böhme where he would talk about Tuesday. The place on the shelf was empty; the work had been left lying open on the windowsill. I had an easy time identifying a few pages farther along:

But then Mars . . .

The count's cane was drawing closer.

. . . and that burning fright . . .

I quickly slipped the volume back into its place on the shelf.

"You put it back where it belongs, fine."

Together we walked down a few steps. He showed me a small room near the entrance, a cell, with a window looking out on the courtyard, a desk, a chair, a cot with a straw mattress and army blankets.

"You'll be able to move in here. This is where professors work who have research to do in the library. At this time there aren't any."

Then he explained something about the light switch, security precautions, obligations toward the Natural Monuments Department and insurance companies. I pretended to listen, I was transported. He closed the door behind me, we were back by the wall; it was almost completely dark. A patch of pink still lingered at the top of certain towers. Lower, a few lighted windows.

It was pitiful to see the way the count was limping. His children and a few others were in a circle, singing and shouting.

"They're playing Witch Hunt."

The voice of the countess announced dinner. Then the children said their good nights. We had our glass of beer and moved into the salon. I helped the count into his armchair. He asked me whether I knew any solitaire games; I remembered one called How to Succeed:

"First, you need to find a two to act as a priest . . ."

"The two of spades."

"A Jesuit; you're in luck, he can perform four weddings before going back into the deck."

"Four weddings?"

"And four christenings. A young man (three) must marry a young maiden (five) richer than he is, always of a different suit . . ."

"By the way, don't you have anything to read? It's rather odd to ask such a question here of all places. But I think you'll also be in the mood for a few more modern works . . . Here's my first wedding."

"The Jesuit stays until the baby arrives, a four, the same suit as his father."

"I personally don't have much to speak of here. My books have remained in trunks, because I don't plan on remaining in my uncle's service forever. Beside the *Almanach de Gotha* . . ."

(the latest numbers of which, as a matter of fact, filled almost an entire small bookcase beside my bed)

"The two of diamonds."

"A Franciscan; he can perform two weddings before going back to the convent. Once the boy is baptized, the priest can be of use elsewhere, and the woman withdraws; you put her back into the deck."

"One day soon we'll go down to a bookstore and find something . . ."

"I brought *Joseph in Egypt*."

"In German?"

"No, French."

"Do you know how to play the solitaire version?"

"The solitaire version?"

"The game called Joseph in Egypt, I'll show you one evening. What happens now?"

"The boy (a four) can seduce a woman (six), a priest can marry them . . ."

"The two of clubs."

"A secular clergyman. He can perform just one wedding before going back to his care."

"What's the heart?"

"Dominican."

"It'll do me good as well to look at more recent writing. Since my arrival I've been so immersed in the period of the Holy Empire . . . A woman (six), married."

"She must wait for a boy (five)."

"But for this evening we'll be able to turn up some sort of detective novel in my bedroom . . ."

"And so on, until the jack marries the queen in order to give birth to a king who conquers the ace."

On the fireplace mantle stood a flask full of an amber liquid.

4

The Student Maiden

"What are you? A man or a vampire?"

She spoke a refined, fluent French.

"I am a man, and I have no dealings whatsoever with vampires!"

She wore a robe of a celestial color.

"By what adventure," she began with a great sigh, caressing with her hand the round glass face of a barometer, "do you find yourself here? I have been in this place for seven times seven weeks, and in all that time you are the first man I've seen."

Her large blue-black eyes, her gentleness, and her open welcome emboldened me to say to her:

"Madame, before I have the honor of satisfying your curiosity, permit me to say that I am infinitely grateful for this unforeseen meeting, which affords me the opportunity to perhaps increase your happiness."

I related to her by what strange accident it was that she saw in my person a student of the University of Paris, the state in which I appeared in her presence—my outfit, an apprentice assistant forester, already torn in places; my faded blue sash and my black boots spattered with muddy snow; my face and hands encrusted with dirt, along with my prominent cheekbones—and how chance brought me to discover the entrance to her magnificent *(though by all appearances tedious) prison.*

"Alas, young Frenchman," she said, sighing again and drawing a veil of resplendent silver around her shoulders, "you are right in thinking that this prison, so rich and resonant, does not escape being an exceedingly tedious abode."

Eyes orange and azure, she slowly spun a lunar globe all the while with one finger nonchalantly flipping through the Parmenides.

"It is impossible that you have never heard of the great Fulcanelli, rector of the University of Figures, thus named because of his precious enigmas, which he produces so abundantly; I am his daughter. With a wink of his golden eye he consented to my marriage with a doctoral candidate, a companion of mine, but on the very night of our wedding, in the midst of the festivities of the faculty of the entire University of Figures, before I had retired with my husband, I was kidnapped by a vampire with azure eyes ringed with alternating orange and black circles."

She had a buckle of blue and azure enamel, with figures of a man and a woman wearing orange robes, carrying scrolls.

"I swooned at that very moment, and, when I had recovered my senses, I found myself in this domain. I was inconsolable for the longest time; but time and necessity have accustomed me to suffering the presence of the vampire."

Her eyes had turned citrine white and iron blue.

"I had in abundance everything that a student who loves nothing but clothes and jewelry could dream of. From week to week the vampire came and spent a night with me; not often, for his wife is very jealous. But if I had need of him, day or night, as soon as I touched the switch at the entrance to my chamber he would appear. It has been four days since he was last here, and I do not expect him for another three, so you may stay with me for two if

you wish, and I shall attempt to entertain you according to your scholarly accomplishments and merit."

She ushered me into the most spotless, most commodious, and most sumptuous bathing chambers; emerging, I donned a perfectly fitted robe of citrine white bordered with gold.

Seated on a settee upholstered with the supple leaves of tender shrubbery with supporting cushions of the most beautiful brocade from the Holy Empire, we tasted together the most delicate dishes, passing the remainder of the day most agreeably, and in the evening she received me in her bed.

As she tried every means to please me the next day, she served at dinner a bottle of Tokay, and, mixing it with furtive tears, she drank a few mouthfuls from my own glass. The wine having gone to our heads:

"Lovely student," I said to her, "for too long have you been buried alive; follow me, come enjoy the sounds of the real towns of which you have been deprived for weeks on end. Abandon the artificial hum that you enjoy here."

"My young Frenchman," she replied with a smile, her eyes turning orange and gold as she spun nervously a globe of the planet Mars on its iron axis, "the world's most beautiful cities would all mean nothing to me, if only you would grant me six days of each week and cede Sunday to the vampire."

"Lovely student, it is fear, I see, that makes you say such things. But I for one have so little fear of him that I am going to smash to pieces this switch with the word MARANATHA written above it. I vow to ridicule everything in the world that has to do with vampires!"

"Such action will cause us to lose each other, you and I; for I know vampires . . ."

But the effects of the Tokay prevented me from appreciating the reasons of the student with eyes of black and white like the moon . . .

5

𝕸𝖎𝖓𝖊𝖗𝖆𝖑𝖔𝖌𝖞

The count's leg was much better by Wednesday; he drank a little more, supported himself with his cane, which he had continued to use for several weeks, but could walk almost as quickly as I.

When entering the upper wall, passing through the portcullis and under the head of the last wolf, one first came upon the guardhouse on the right, which was also a restaurant, or more precisely, a refreshment stand. The castle was on a popular tourist route, "The Romantic Way," and the guard doubled as guide and served wine or beer or apple juice to go with the bread and sausages brought along by those who had planned ahead.

The count introduced me to him (dressed like a forester, in black with a gray jacket, green in back, buttons of bone or rather bronze with the prince's coat of arms), assuring me that he would be entirely at my disposal, except during official visiting hours, to open every door, and the count asked him to hand over the enormous bunch of keys.

He too was a refugee; he had been one of the count's people in the Sudentenland. Then came a large rectangular two-story building, two-toned shutters, with a tower enclosing a spiral staircase.

The ground floor consisted of one immense, vaulted

hall, in which diverse collections had been somewhat randomly accumulated.

"The princes of O— W—," the count explained to me,

(the W— needs to be added because there are two other families of O— who, centuries ago, had detached themselves from the trunk of the familial tree common to them—you can look it up in the *Gotha*—and the present prince, owner of all this, my wife's uncle, personally resides at W—, another of his seven palaces—I shall perhaps take you there one of these days)

"reigned as monarchs over the region until Napoleon reunited their territories with the kingdom of Bavaria. In the eighteenth century, having nothing much to do, they all became avid collectors, each racking his brain to discover a category of collectibles that had not interested his predecessors; for that reason, one came up with the idea of collecting all these buttons, another these fossils,

(a plaster cast of the skeleton of an ichthyosaur behind cracked glass)

"but mainly there is this enormous collection of minerals,

(yellow gray zircons running through monazites, zigzagging aragonites)

"dusty, in disorder, we haven't had time to arrange any of this,

(he blew on the arborescent argentites, the vitreous bronzites, the brown wolframites from Portugal)

"which is not very spectacular, the specimens are rarely cut larger than a nut,

(he dusted off barites lying like open books, efflorescent cinnabars, rhombohedron dolomites, blue vivianites)

"but some of them are, they say, quite precious,"

(holding up to the light some cassiterites, somber green enstatites, replacing them in the cardboard compartments on the tables

—cube-shaped fluorites, emerald green uvarovites, nacre diaspores—

with small labels on which the names had been written out by hand:
grossularites, black hornblendes, turquoises from Nishapur, murky eleolites,
but by what hand, at what time, in what language?)
—red and yellow idocrases, green jaspers;
names soaring for me
—spinels set side by side in octahedrals, feldspars within carlsbad twins, kieselguhrs—
like moths
—ruby lepidocrocite micas, crowns of rutile, dovetailed gypsums, bluish green moroxites—
on these tiny tarnished stones.
This room did not appear on the tourists' route; in the middle there was a large door standing wide open, and it was from there that daylight shone
on the greenish nitratines, smoked quartzes from Uri;
there were numerous windows, but the shutters were almost always closed. Above
—but we had to leave, carefully close the double door, lock it, climb the spiral staircase in the adjacent tower—
in several rooms, the schoolmaster from the village below had been allowed to display his remarkable collection of painted Bavarian armoires.
Then, following the parapet walk, we reached the oldest tower, called the Thieves, which had no door on the ground level, no windows to speak of, only a few narrow loopholes,
somber gray, with a roof that formed an oblique trapezium,
dating, it was said, from the eleventh century.
It was the torture chamber: oubliettes and very small cells, in which one could neither stand nor lie down (as in the *fillettes* of our Louis XI), with a peephole for confessions and curtains to encourage confidences.
Back to the parapet walk, then to the tower of the Knights' Chamber, on the same floor as the count's

apartment. By the broad stairway that occupied the next wide, adjacent tower, the Rotten—square, the roof forming a flattened bulb—we mounted to that vast chamber of the eighteenth century, the brightest of all the castle rooms with its thirteen high windows, and the most ornate, with its two stucco fireplaces, and its ceiling framing nine paintings:

Mercury at the south end,

a horn in the corner with an inscription in French:

He leads and spurs on the hunt,

War at the east, Medea at the north, Peace at the west,

a guard dog, a vulture seizing a hare, and a wild boar in the corners with their inscriptions,

Perseus freeing Andromeda in the center,

housing a collection of thirty thousand prints arranged in the long drawers of beautiful, polished cabinets on which one could spread them in order to study them as one wished.

On the floor below, under our floor, another apartment in which another of the prince's relations lived with her daughter. One never saw them, one preferred not to mention them; at least one of them went out from time to time to do the shopping, but ever so discreetly. Two shadows, two gazes divined rather than perceived in the dusk behind the pane, when a lone window was illumined.

In the shadow of the library, a small walled garden with some garden chairs and tables, several fruit trees, a vine, I think, a swing.

In the center, a deep well.

On the other side of the ravine's mouth, by the portal, the portcullis, the head of the last wolf, at the bottom of the kitchen garden (which the guard's wife tended), a small, half-timbered house, the roof of which did not reach above the parapet walk, "the witch's house"; here lived another old woman, the domestic of someone in the family, she too swept here by the squall of history.

Then the "bakery," with its spiral staircase, the interior in ruins, under restoration, a passageway surmounting three arcades to join it to the library, formerly called the Prince's Tower, and behind it, the seventeenth-century church, all black and white inside, with an organ of the period, littered with small scaffolds, cords, and sacks of plaster, all the flagstones pulled and piled up,

its crypt with the remains of the O— W— family, its small court, its bell tower.

After lunch, the count gave me a key to the Prince's Tower, saying:

"Now you will be able to enter here whenever you like."

I prepare myself for an orgy of deciphering. I quietly enter the immense building.

A clock. Completely alone, I follow the shelves of rough wood, climb ladders; paper dust, bindings of old parchment, dryness of leaves, crackling of backs . . . The gleam of Dialectic . . . A murmur . . . and in the *Tripus Aureus, hoc est Tres Tractatus Chymici Selectissimi* reprinted in the *Musæum Hermeticum,* I stumbled through:

Mars is expert in the things of war and exercises a certain power by way of the *ardor igneous,*

a humming . . .

and for him, Geometry spreads a blood-drenched veil on which one sees Strength draped in red . . .

A droning . . .

I ascended to the rotunda:

. . . I raised my foot and administered to the alcove a mighty kick—and Shahrazad perceived the dawn of day . . .

(and I imagine hypersthenic eyes),

. . . "With joy and goodly gree," answered Shahrazad. The Sultan . . .

(onyx eyes),

the droning swells . . .

. . . "By Allah, I will not slay her, until I have heard the rest of her tale" the next night Dunyazad . . .

(pitchblendes),
swells as though a huge machine has been activated . . .

. . . said to her sister Shahrazad . . .

whines louder . . .

. . . of the two others . . .

louder, invading . . .

my dear sister . . .

becomes piercing, unbearable, like a conflagration of noise breaking out; I bound down the stairs four at a time, dash into the cell, open the window, the noise is even louder, it invades the entire sky. Is it war, another war . . .

A great commotion in the courtyard. All kinds of people running together in total panic. I recognize the guard at the head of the crowd. He comes toward the library; I go down to meet him. He opens the door. There are twenty people behind him, menacing.

"Oh, it's you!"

"What's going on?"

Without answering he walks up a few steps, passing me, and pushes a switch. The noise dies down, away, peters out, a kind of irritated death rattle, several hiccups, and it is over.

He explained something to the people with him, and to others coming through the portcullis. They disperse.

I had set off the alarm. It was the sort of siren that went off automatically when someone opened the first door; it had to be cut off by a hidden button before it became audible. The count had evidently explained all this to me the day before, but amidst all the paintings, the stained-glass windows, the tapestries, and all those books . . .

After that experience I knew that the silence of my cell was like a fragile bridge over a chasm of pandemonium. This entire castle was a bubble in time, miraculously spared from the flames, an island in time, with shores, with fortresses built up by the tides, the waves of the present, an island that had provided shelter for all the survivors from another part of the Holy Empire, from another bubble in time which itself had expired under the madness.

Ah, the door must be locked and barred! The iridescent walls were so thin! I had my ears peeled for the slightest whisper; while trying to find my way through the Latin or German sentences, I felt a sudden pang of anguish on being reminded of that noise which shared similarities with all the sirens of the preceding years. Whether what I was hearing was an airplane flying over us (it had to be an American one at that time and place), or even a gust of wind carrying the sound of a train or truck echoing off the prison tower into the court, I stopped my reading, I waited, looked out the window, all was calm, the grass, the witch's house, someone was drinking something in the guard's hut, silence, I strolled through the tunnels of forgotten controversies, of terrifying marvels, of heraldry, alchemy, exorcisms, all was calm, I returned to my cell, resumed my slow reading of the *Practica cum Duodecim Clavibus & Appendice, de Magno Lapide Antiquorum Sapientium, cripta & relicta,* printed in *The Golden Tripod:*

Mercury possesses the powers of a chancellor before whom Arithmetic holds an iridescent banner upon which marvelous hues represent Temperance,

or that of Father Kircher's *Iter Extaticum:*

—and under the guidance of the archangel Uriel, I steeped myself in the music of the spheres, I leaped to the Moon and to Mars and to Mercury—

or even plunging into his book on the *Obelisks of Rome* or into his *Œdipus Ægyptiacus,* following him, I pictured a whole baroque and sententious Nile

—O Father Kircher, you were truly my Virgil in the exploration of this sunken world!—

or else I devoured that French work from the eighteenth century, the astonishing precursor of the famous treatise by Hervey Saint-Denys, *Dreams and the Means to Direct Them,* in bound leaves without a cover, or author's name, *The Art of Finding Happiness Through Dreams,* which opened with a brilliant defense and illustration of the role of dreams in our lives, then provided three drug mixtures to be swallowed or inhaled before sleep in order to obtain each desired dream (and what dreams!), each recipe drawn from one of the three natural orders, for example, concoctions with various bases, of pyrite, eagle feathers, or dandelion, for visiting the planet Mars. Back in Paris, I talked to all sorts of people who had dreamt of reading this book, especially Dr. H—, who went hunting for it during one of his subsequent trips to Franconia, and who told me that he had not been able to find a trace of it in the card catalogue, and that I must have dreamt having read the book of dreams (but no doubt someone will turn it up in some large library, or plainly and simply in its place in the castle).

As soon as I set foot in the building, I ever so carefully pushed that red button which alone protected me from the hellish clamoring, the sudden transformation of the peaceful inhabitants of the two neighboring towns into a sneering mob full of hatred.

That evening, the count decided to win at Witch Hunt.

I thumbed through a book I had found in the small bookshelves at the head of my sofa bed, almost the latest number of the *Almanach de Gotha,* on the subject of, or rather against the idea of modern art (both author and title have slipped my mind), but which was interesting because it brought together for the first time certain

recent works of several French architects from the end
of the eighteenth century, in particular Ledoux and
Boullée, whose sublime project of a monument to Newton
I discovered, a sphere replicating the night sky, where a
glowing sun is surrounded by its entire solar system.

The witch was the queen of clubs,

whom I had always called Argine, but who in his version took the name Cleopatra in German characters,

whom he had to surround with a circle made of all the
children (all the cards with the exception of the face
cards and aces).

In the count's hands the clubs seemed to me to turn
into iron crosses of pyrite, the spades into indigolites on
silver plate.

While placing the jacks (men-at-arms) at the four corners of the witch to guard her

—but the "loose women," the three other queens, could
entice them away, lead them back into the deck after
them—

he reminisced to me about the Russian campaign: the
snow, the wind, the mud.

Above my bed his brother, standing in his portrait.

"As long as the witch is not guarded on all sides by the
men-at-arms, Satan, the king of clubs, may free her; he
leads her out of the circle and the whole game starts over
again."

In his hands the diamonds became helicoidal quartz,
the hearts, rhodocrosites on iron plate.

A bell somewhere.

And he spoke to me about gun battles on the snow.

Once the circle was completely closed, the "loose
women" repented; he placed them on top to pray for the
soul of their sister.

I thought:

"Since the count has not offered me a taste of the contents of the flask on the mantelpiece, perhaps it isn't for
drinking, perhaps it's some perfume . . ."

Once the witch fell under the complete control of the four men-at-arms in the middle of the closed circle, Satan went back down to his hell below; the count lit the pyre with the ace of diamonds, stoked it with the heart, stirred it with the spade, spread the ashes with the ace of clubs; at this moment the sky opened, and he aligned the last three kings at the very top to represent the trinity.

6

The Forester

An appalling stench dispelled the fumes in a matter of minutes.

"Lovely student," I cried, "what does this mean?"

"Alas, you are lost if you do not run for your life."

Having gathered up my apprentice's outfit as fast as I could

—though my horror was so great I forgot my boots and stylus—

I was just about to set foot on the stairs by which I had descended when the philosophic abode opened and made a passageway for the vampire with the golden eyes surrounded by circles of blue, and of white as the clubs of Mercury.

Dressed in the completely citrine white uniform of an officer, with buttons of iron cross-shaped pyrite and a cloak embroidered with a figure of Alexander holding a naked glaive with Lancelot kneeling at his feet, he angrily asked the student in her red robe:

"What has happened to you, and why have you summoned me?"

To my great astonishment, he addressed her in a refined, fluent French.

"I felt a queasiness in my stomach," she replied, leafing with mock nonchalance through one of Euclid's works, *while toying nervously with the antique alcoholometer which she had made into a brooch, and her eyes turned white and green, "and so I reached for the bottle which you can see. I had taken two or three swallows; as ill luck would have it, I stumbled and fell against the button, which shattered. Nothing more."*

At this reply the vampire, his eyes black, white, orange:
"You are a bald-faced liar! Look at those boots and stylus, what are they doing here?"

"This is the first time I've set eyes on them," replied the student, leafing with mock nonchalance through a work by Diophantus, while leaning against a column of cinnabar and swiveling on its stand the globe of the planet Mercury, and her eyes took on violet and citrine white hues. "Perhaps in your haste to come here, you brushed past them and unwittingly carried them along with you."

Her iridescent scarf quivered in her trembling fingers.

An organ sounded a trill in an adamantine second played with argentine technique.

The vampire, his eyes green and citrine white, white as the spades of the moon, answered her only with insults and blows whose force I could feel.

Her veil was bloody, her torn dress revealed the marvelous hues of her undergarments.

Quickly I stripped off the dressing gown (citrine white with gold trim) and slipped into my apprentice assistant forester's uniform. Thus I reached the surface, but my remorse and compassion were all the more overwhelming, for by sacrificing the most beautiful student in the world to the barbarity of the implacable vampire, I had become a criminal and the most ungrateful wretch on earth.

Once the trapdoor was lowered, and re-covered with snow, and I myself was back in Budapest so troubled and afflicted I didn't know what I was doing, the very elderly man, dressed in purple from head to toe, was overjoyed to see me again:

"*Your absence,*" *he said to me,* "*worried me greatly, because of the secret about your studies which you confided to me. I was full of all sorts of thoughts and feared that someone had found you out. May the Lord be praised for your safe return!*"

I thanked him for his zeal and his affection, but chose not to pass on anything that had happened to me, or the reason why I had come back without my boots.

On my cot in his consulting room, I reproached myself for my excessive foolhardiness:

"*Nothing would have been able to match the student's happiness and my own if I had only been able to restrain myself . . .*"

While I surrendered to these distressing reflections, my host entered:

"*A master forester whom I do not know, his eyes orange as Tokay with inner rings blue as the diamonds of Mercury one instant, and the next violet, has just arrived with your stylus and your boots, which he found along his path, according to his story. He learned that you lived here from the companions who walk with you in the Black Forest: come speak with him, he wishes to return them to you personally.*"

From the organ, a trill in a metallic second played with cinnabar technique.

On hearing these words, I changed color and began to tremble in every limb. When the very elderly man asked me the reason, the floor of the consultation room opened, and the forester appeared, his eyes dark violet, orange, citrine red, in his green uniform with the four buttons made of bone on which were set

a tine of zircon, a guard dog of wolframite, a vulture of blue vivianite seizing a hare of emerald green uvarovite, and a wild board of turquoise from Nishapur.

"*I am a vampire,*" *he told us,* "*son of the daughter of Nosferatu, rector of vampires. Is this not your stylus here? Are these not also your boots?*"

He did not give me time to answer, nor would I have been able to, for his presence was so ghastly I had become frantic. He grabbed me by my waist, dragged me out of the consultation chamber, and unfolding huge webbed wings, his face turned into a wall-dwelling falcon's, and he swept me off into the sky with such force and speed that soon the planet Mars was before my eyes with its plains of pyrites and marcassites, its monuments shaped like iron crosses, pentagonical dodecahedrons, spectacular rosettes, cockscombs, clusters of spears.

He swooped straight toward the ground and, with a stamp of his boots, he opened it up and dived inside.

I found myself back in the philosophic abode before the beautiful student of the University of Figures, but alas, what a sight! Naked, covered with blood, stretched upon the flagstones, more dead than alive, and her cheeks bathed in tears.

"False-hearted woman," said the vampire to her, "is this not your lover?"

And on the button that grew around the tine, I saw glowing in letters of spinel

He leads and spurs on the hunt.

She cast me a languishing gaze and sorrowfully replied:

"I do not know him; this is the first time I have ever set eyes on him."

. . . on the button growing around the dog, glowing in letters of rutile:

Do not lay me here.

"What," replied the vampire, "he is the reason for your present condition, which you so richly deserve, and you dare say . . ."

growing around the vulture, glowing in letters of smoky quartz:

On the point of victory.

"If I do not know him," the student retorted, "do you want me to tell a lie which will cost him his life?"

. . . around the wild boar in letters of pyrite:

He is good only after death.

"Well then," the vampire said, taking from an orpiment casket a crossbow with a nephelite hilt, "if you have never seen him, then take this and shoot him in the head!"

And on the button which kept growing around the tine, I saw glowing in marcassite:

Homo veniet ad judicium vampiri.

"Alas," the student said, "how could I do what you ask of me? My strength is so exhausted that I cannot lift my arm; and, even if I could, would I find it in my heart to kill an innocent man?"

. . . continuing to grow around the dog, glowing in letters of limonite:

Vere illa dies terribilis erit.

Then the vampire told the student: "This refusal reveals the full extent of your crime to me. And what have you to say?"

"How could I know her, since this is the first and only time I have set eyes on her . . ."

. . . still growing around the vulture, in very clear letters of kliachites:

O rex sempiterne.

"If this is so," the vampire replied, "then take this crossbow and shoot her in the head. This is the price I set for your freedom . . ."

"With pleasure," I rejoined . . .

. . . still, still growing around the boar, still, in lovely and very clear letters of Ceylonese jargoon:

Dele verba quae dixi.

7

The Parapet Walk

The countess's elegance, her bearing, with such nobility, such ease in her air, the kind, open welcome she extended to me, with that look in her eyes . . .

The upper wall was elliptical, the parapet walk tile-roofed; all the woodwork and the guardrails had been wonderfully preserved; it was especially remarkable for its adjustable loopholes that could be used for targeting arrows from a bow or crossbow, made of huge wooden spheres pierced by a cylindrical aperture wide enough to allow a hand to be easily inserted, and which you could turn inside their circular casing; some were blocked by dirt build-ups, but most still functioned perfectly; indeed the opportunity to work them around came up often enough: with each group of passing tourists, that is to say, almost daily during the summer a few were demonstrated.

Through a few breaches you could see a vast stretch of the horizon: the village below, wedged in the gorge on both banks of the river W— and, on the other side, in the distance, several other villages, surrounded by forests or fields; in one spot a cement factory, half hidden, whose gray clouds of dust were visible by day, and by night its fiery glow.

These loopholes, these targeting spheres served me as

a telescope, as optical weapons; I spent a long time using each, hours upon hours, like a bowman of old, on the lookout, surveying like an astronomer, but more similar to Tycho Brahe at Uranienburg than a present-day researcher, in my efforts to carve out circular swaths from the countryside, the pill-shapes of roofs, paving stones, meadows, woods, clouds, towns, bubbles of German air, German colors, so that I would be able to take them away with me on other impending trips I had decided upon, but whose itineraries or destinations were still unknown, here capturing a person passing by, or a shadow, or a bird.

Expanses of sunshine, of rolling hills whose borders, currents and nodes I was thus able to determine, large reserves of shade and coolness, gulfs of reflections and of torpor, gentle crystalline cloudbursts, pools of transparency, quiverings, approaching storms, the cries of animals, or human sounds.

I had the impression the whole scene was orchestrated by the hand of an artist, none of whose paintings I had ever seen, just some black and white reproductions in magazines, a painter of delicate inspiration, obsessive, with a feel for ghostly nuance, bathed in a light inexhaustibly gradated, nostalgic, shimmering in the intense heat, whose name had slipped my mind.

"A painter," I said to the count, "you're surely familiar with him, a Romantic: Frédéric, Carl David, Gustav David, Friedreich Gaspard David, or something like that . . ."

And naturally he told me the name, but the next day, with the landscape before me, it started to shift around again, to taunt me.

I began to explore the region, first by proceeding to the next two railway stations: N—, with its castle wall, a larger version of the one found at the castle of H—; and D—, with a former Benedictine abbey that had been converted into a school, and joined in the past (so it was whispered about) to a Claretian convent by underground passageways unearthed at the turn of the century, where the bones of adults and children alike were discovered.

Close by stood the home of Alexander von B—. The very evening I arrived, I informed the count about the task with which I had been commissioned by Doctor H—. He had the precious package delivered by a cyclist from the village below. In return we were invited to tea.

It was a tiny, charming castle, country baroque, like the apartment where we lived at H— in the tower of the Knights' Chamber, painted in ocher with white trim, a small French garden in front, and an English one in the rear.

Alexander von B— was an old German of great elegance, whose features reminded me of Max Ernst, an aquiline nose, pale blue eyes, white hair swept back from both sides of a high forehead. His wife, much younger than he, had been a soprano before their marriage, and retained a Maeterlinckesque quality, long pale hair, a dress of reed-green silk; she seemed to pass from room to room without her feet touching the ground.

On the door to the dining room hung a harp, or rather a zither with horizontal strings across which, every time the door opened or somebody walked past, a small metal ball on a string bounced up, then back, rebounded, rolled, swayed for the longest time, producing delicate arpeggios, faint trills, melodious vibrations that lasted a while, then died away, and which among the castle's residents had inspired an entire art of entrances and exits: everyone had their own techniques, their figures, and each woman especially knew how to surround each of her appearances or disappearances with a floating murmur, like a thick mane of sounds, rippling, crystalline, drawn out, which heightened, singled out, prolonged the movements of her proud, beautiful, weary face, her beautiful, faraway eyes.

They had a daughter, about sixteen years old, still treated as though she were six, who reigned, in a small room between storeys furnished with miniature furniture, over a population of dolls.

There was also Sebastien P—, a young architect, the son of another writer, whom Alexander von B— had adopted after his father died, and who lived there, in the attic, in order to successfully complete a huge novel, though whether it was ever published I don't know.

The master of the house gave us a glimpse of his laboratory, then before tea, recited to us a poem by Verlaine (he spoke a refined, fluent, old-fashioned French), and, switching to English, one by Robert Frost.

He took me aside to thank me for delivering *The Philosophic Abodes* and, nodding his noble head, disclosed to me that this Fulcanelli must have known something.

Upon our return the count said to me:

"Here is a small work which might interest you. It will make a good souvenir. I have only a few copies left."

Gray, in Gothic characters, undated, with a few blurry photographs, and the title: *The Castle of H—*.

"You'll find information on its construction, its owners, the celebrations held there, and even the executions."

"The executions?"

"That's right, the capital executions; of course, the names of the majority of those imprisoned in the adjoining tower, or at a later time, inside the other one that surmounts the guardhouse, have vanished in the mists of time. Our lists date back only as far as 1662, take a look: Georg Stengler d'Ebernergen, executed by sword, then burnt at the stake. Then we jump to 1665, which doesn't mean that between the two dates there wasn't . . . Stephen Greissing of Salzbourg, for theft, caned, one ear cut off; 1666, Eva Erber, guard of the upper castle door— that means she had been a jailer, a single wall separated her prison cell from her former bedchamber, for sundry adulteries, executed by sword . . .

And I found again my orpiments from Hungary, my red jaspers, the shelves of geometry and *The First Book of Moses Explained:*

On the fourth day, Mercury . . .

(somewhere a bell tolled in the key of G)

the whole firmament is like a fading resonance . . .

(my footsteps echoing along the shelves)

A king, and if I may be permitted the comparison, a natural god, with six councillors, the Sun . . .

In the Knights' Chamber I studied Dürer's *Melancholy* and ancient cards from India, walked up to the rotunda:

. . . taking the sword went forward sharply and raised my hand to smite Sharazad halted at this spot . . .

(to me she resembled Strength, clothed in red, with eyes of blue schorl)

. . . perceived the dawn of day my sister said Dunyazad . . .

(to me she resembled Prudence, clothed in a celestial hue, with her eyes of pearly talc)

. . . I am enchanted by this tale which so agreeably holds my attention if the Sultan allows me to live today . . .

(resembling the god Mars, fiery and furious, with his nephelite eyes).

And from the top of the uppermost windows of the turret, in the room housing the souvenirs of the War of 1870, while the wall-dwelling falcons were screeching, I could sometimes see, on the rising hill, children older than those dancing in circles and playing witch hunt on the inside, who were putting on long historical fairy tale-like dramas, using curtains for costumes, not one word of which I could make out,

. . . And where is this compared with what I could tell thee on the coming night if the King deign spare my life. Shahryar, curious to discover . . .

coming as much from *The Thousand and One Nights* as the Bible,

. . . what would befall the Princess of the Ebony Islands and her lover . . .

for this king could be a Pharaoh or Shahryar, this queen the wife of Potiphar or Scheherazade, this minister the grand vizier or the grand cupbearer, these brothers the three Kalandars or Joseph's tormentors.

One day, all the shutters of the mineral room were opened, the tables holding the cardboard boxes, with their fossils and buttons, their lens of kernite, ulexites, resinous vesuvianites, eurite marcasites, set in rows, pushed against the walls; long planks on trestles had been set up for the banquet of the association of German nobility whose president was Prince von O— W—.

The latter, dressed as a forester (in point of fact he was the owner not only of seven castles, but of seven forests), gave his guests a tour of the parapet walk, showed them how the wooden balls swiveled around in the loopholes, led them over to the Treasure House for a glance at the ivory Christ and the Irish manuscript, lying among the books on the Franconian tapestries and the statue of Tilman Riemenschneider, then showed them to their seats for lunch.

Certainly the lapis lazuli, the wiluites from eastern Siberia, amassed by his ancestors, were safe and secure; the German nobility recounted their family histories; now they were skimming all the pages of the *Almanach de Gotha.*

Especially a few very old persons, evidently penniless for the most part, refugees from East Germany, Siberia, Bohemia, dreaming about their lost castles, their collections, their people, their lands, their relatives remaining behind, dressed in the shabbiest cloth, but decked with the most sumptuous ancient jewels, stones, polished, washed, sparkling amid their softly glowing gold,

old people clinking, wizened, their necks, their backs bolt upright, their fingers stretched to raise glasses for the toasts,

all those stones shimmering against that background of sleeping stones . . .

Sometime later, on a Thursday, I accompanied the count to the castle of W—, belonging to the branch of the von O—'s that had given the prince his name. It was his main residence, but that day he was not there; it was his sister, the countess's mother, who received us.

Enormous yellow-painted barracks with a charming Directory-style wing built for a dowager princess, long corridors lined with family portraits, a certain number of other collections installed there, the usable collections, or those having special sentimental value: porcelains, glass jewelry, silhouettes.

We were shown into a high-ceilinged room where a group of ten or so ladies were sewing, conversing, occupying themselves; but, for lunch, we numbered just three: the countess B—, the count, and myself, only three "masters," for behind each chair there stood

—Dresden china, crystal, silverware, polished wood under lace—

a valet in livery and powdered wig attached to each neck with a bow. Here we had to speak French so that they wouldn't understand. The view on the trees in the park.

The coffee was served outside. Sandy ground, it seems to me that we were in the shade of a large plane tree; already, on the lawn, a few fallen leaves. A valet in livery rolls out a table.

The Countess B—, in a sprightly mood, takes out of her bag an elongated leather case, opens it, and offers me a huge cigar which I accept, dumbfounded.

"I have far greater surprises in store for you."

And taking another, she immediately lights up.

Parapet walk, fibrous zeolites, honey yellow wulfenites . . .

In the Knights' Chamber I studied the landscapes of Hercule Seghers and ancient maps of China, skimmed the shelves of arithmetic, and went back over to sit in the cell in order to fly away in the arms of the archangel Uriel as far as the cinnabar plains of the planet Mercury, or to decipher a little bit more quickly the fourteenth chapter of the *Mysterium Magnum,* the commentary on verses 20-32 in the first book of Moses:

. . . in the four elements, the four firmaments, the creatures of the earth, birds of the air, fish . . .

(a troop of tourists were climbing the Tower of the Staircase adjoining the mineralogy collection),

. . . the fifth day, Jupiter . . .

(then moved along the parapet walk to go visit the Torture Tower),

. . . and as one sees that fire cannot burn without water and that water without fire would be nothing . . .

(and the shadows climbed along the towers),

thus each of the two sexes cannot deprive itself of the other and each violently pines for its complement . . .

(and the children shouted in their witch hunts),

or amuse myself in the pages of *The Art of Finding Happiness Through Dreams* with those preparations made of various bases, cassiterite, sempervivium, or eagle claws, in order to dream that you have been transformed into the animal of your choice.

In the evening, after dinner, sometimes I joined the count on the moor overlooking the red glowing cement factory. Its sounds, the last village sounds: shutters being closed, a train perhaps, a car. Above us, the summer

constellations. He had a few words to say to the dog
trainer, who used this ground as his exercise field with
his whistles and whips, about the huge magnificent
growling beasts that belonged to the prince.

Then he taught me how to play Joseph in Egypt:

"First, you build the house, stone by stone, four taper-
ing columns from the nine to the ace, and the ten at the
summit to stand for the capitals . . ."

I thought to myself, while looking at the flask on the
fireplace mantel: maybe it's plainly and simply some
drug, some embrocation . . .

"You set yourself up in the center room, Potiphar with
his fan (a spade), his wife to the left, and Joseph his
slave to the right, with the others, male and female . . ."

In my hand I was holding *Star of the Unborn* by Franz
Werfel, one of the oldest friends of Alexander von B—,
and which the count had gone to buy down at the village
bookstore with me in mind.

"Madame Potiphar wants to seduce her Joseph, but
she dares act only after her husband is called out by an
important person: Pharaoh with his scepter, the great
cupbearer with his heart-shaped ewer, the great pantler
with his square plate. Then she passes into the center
bedroom, dismisses the servants one by one . . ."

I thought: perhaps it's some hair lotion that the countess has mislaid and is looking for . . .

"Joseph flees from her, hides on the other side of the
house. And now Potiphar comes back. She accuses the
Jewish boy: 'He's just left my bedroom, can't you see,
that's my fan he's holding in his hand . . .' "

I used my index finger as a bookmarker.

"With the three jacks I make two prison cells where I
lock up the grand officers, each guarded by a soldier of
the same suit, and I place Joseph, falsely accused, above
the jack of spades in the middle . . ."

A bell.

"I destroy the house of Potiphar in order to build the

Pharaoh's palace, keeping aside the three which I place above the grand officers in their prison, representing their dreams: vine twigs (spades), grape bunches (hearts), baskets (diamonds), birds (clubs), flanking Joseph who is going to interpret them for him, the sevens that will come later, flanking the crown on the Pharaoh in the throne room, thick and thin black ears of grain, red cows . . ."

I thought: a hair remover . . .

"The ladies of the court in the left nave, the lords to the right. The great cupbearer has ended his favorable dream, he can return to the palace with his guard (a jack), and once the Pharaoh's vision has been completely set out, here, place Joseph in triumph above the figures which he's deciphering . . ."

The silent count then studied the image while arranging in a horizontal row at the foot of the throne

(for me, set with cube-shaped zeolites, malachite concretions . . .)

the cadaver of the king of diamonds guarded by the two jacks, men-at-arms.

8

The Metamorphosis

The student maiden understood my drawing: despite her
pains and her affliction, she signaled her comprehension
with an obliging glance of her citrine white and tin violet
eyes, and made me to understand that she would gladly
die, so happy was she to see that I also wanted to die for
her.

"Clearly I can see," said the vampire, and his eyes had
turned lacquer red, the crimson red of Mercury and Mars,
red, and the buttons of his forester's outfit burned with
roaring flames, "that the pair of you are defying me!"

He grabbed his crossbow out of my hands and shot an
arrow into the throat of the student who had just enough
time to bid me an eternal farewell with her eyes, moon
green and white: for the blood that she had already lost
and which she was then losing robbed her of one further
moment of life beyond this last act of cruelty, the sight of
which made me black out.

After coming around, I complained to the vampire that
he was making me languish in expectation of my death,
but instead of granting me my wish:

"That's the way," he said, his eyes red red red, the lacquer of Mercury and Jupiter, "vampires treat the women
they suspect of infidelity. She has received you!"

From the organ a trill in a glassy third played with

enstatite technique.

"If I was confident that she dishonored me more than she has, I would have you killed on the spot . . ."

Those words gave me some hope of swaying him.

"I'll settle for changing you into a dog."

"O vampire," I said to him, and the circles around his citrine red eyes took on orange or dark violent tints, "temper your anger . . ."

"Or into a wild boar."

"And since you don't want to take my life . . ."

"Or into a vulture."

"Generously grant me that wish."

"Or into a hare."

"I will always remember your mercy if you pardon me in the same way Joseph in Egypt pardoned his brothers who bore him a mortal envy."

"I must make you feel what I am capable of."

Seizing me violently he spread his huge webbed wings and, carrying me up through the opening vault of the philosophic abode, he swept me off to the planet Mercury whose metallic seas, emerald plateaus, monuments to the inventor of the alphabet, and torrid sky flashed past my eyes. Then he bolted earthward like a comet, found a foothold on the summit of a black mountain where he unearthed a device with a cassiterite mirror. With the circles around his violet eyes switching back and forth from blue to orange, he proceeded to make certain adjustments whose meaning totally escaped me. Then he aimed it in my direction:

"Shed," he told me, and from the four incandescent buttons of his forester's outfit gushed fountains of mercury and blood, "your human form and take that of an ape."

Instantly he disappeared, and I stood alone, changed into an ape, flooded with sorrow in an unknown land, not knowing whether I was near or far from the university of my professor mentor.

The flat dry country where I wandered after coming down from the black mountain was strewn with zig-zagging deposits of aragonite and barite exposed to the air, but what did any of that matter to me, the most pearly diaspores, the murkiest elaeolites, the most beautiful twinned crystals of feldspar or gypsum, the glassiest hypersthenes or the most intense indigolites, in the state I found myself in?

Then reaching the shore of a very calm sea I spotted a ship one-half league from land, with a large sail embroidered with three persons who had been raised from the dead, David, Charlemagne, and Pallas, all in white, Judith and Cleopatra above them, and at the very top the figure of Alexander coming to judge the world, wearing an absolutely citrine white robe.

In order not to lose such a favorable opportunity, with my teeth and nails, covering myself with blood, I sawed off a large branch of a hollow oak, rolled it to the water, and placed myself on top, my legs akimbo, a stick in each hand for oars.

When I was near enough to be recognized, all the sailors and tourists who appeared on the upper deck looked upon me in admiration.

After climbing on board along a rope, I found myself in a terrible predicament since I was unable to speak.

The superstitious tourists believed that I would bring bad luck to their sea journey; one said:
"I'm going to shoot him dead with my crossbow."
another:
"I want to stab him through with my stylus."
another:
"We must toss him back into the sea."
And someone most surely would have acted on those words if I hadn't gone over to the captain, a very elderly man with orange eyes the shade of Tokay, and prostrated myself at his feet, grabbing him by his purple uniform, in a supplicant's posture. Touched by the tears he saw

streaming from my eyes, he threatened that anybody who brought me harm would regret it, and he petted me.

Fortunately, after seven weeks a favorable wind following the calm brought us into the port of a very beautiful, teeming city, all the more significant for being the seat of an illustrious university.

On the organ a trill in a pearly third played with grossularite technique.

Our ship was soon surrounded by a countless swarm of small crafts, full of people who had come to congratulate their friends on their arrival, or gather news about those whom they had met in their far-off lands; a few beadles in absolutely citrine white livery, with powdered wigs tied to their necks with a bow, addressed the tourists on board our ship:

"Our master the rector has charged us to express his joy to you on your visit, and to request that you each make the effort to write with an iron stylus, on these leaves of supple bark, a few lines of German writing."

The French they spoke was refined, fluent, old-fashioned, exquisite.

"The recently deceased first secretary, along with a very great ability in the handling of affairs, was also able to write German to absolute perfection. Sorely afflicted, the rector vowed to give his position only to an equally refined calligrapher. However, among the numerous competitors throughout this academy, so far not one has been deemed worthy."

Those tourists who believed they could write this language rather well enough to lay claim to such a high rank, one after another wrote down whatever they chose.

Once they'd ended their attempts, as I had taken a leaf from the man collecting them, each and every one, and most especially those who had just participated in the contest, imagining that I wanted to rip it up or throw it into the sea, the man started to shout loudly. Seeing that I was holding it very properly and was motioning that I wanted to have my turn at writing, their worries were quieted and they began marveling.

Nevertheless, since they had never seen an ape that knew how to write, and since I was unable to persuade them that I was more skilled, they wanted to yank the bark from my hands; the captain intervened:

"Leave him alone! If he starts scribbling I'll punish him on the spot. If, on the contrary, he writes well, as I hope, for I've never in my life seen a more ingenious and clever ape, nor one who had a more complete understanding of everything, I'll acknowledge him as my son. My own son did not have anywhere near so much wit about him."

Seeing that no one opposed my plans any longer, I picked up the stylus and set it down again only after having produced an imitation of the writing of Basil Valentine, Jacob Böhme, Father Athanasius Kircher, Jean-Paul Richter, Hegel, Marx, and Enno Littmann.

9

𝔐𝔲𝔫𝔡𝔲𝔰 𝔖𝔲𝔟𝔱𝔢𝔯𝔯𝔞𝔫𝔢𝔲𝔰

After I spent enough time touching and moving around
the most fascinating stones

(botryoidal limonites, that is, resembling bunches of
grapes, drab pitch-black or brown uranites, inflatable
vermiculites that scale away and buckle when exposed to
heat, milk white nephrites with the same name as the
disease . . .),

often I would leave for the entire afternoon, following a
course in which I cut wide spirals around the castle,
which looked different at every fresh turn, and whose
dark profile stood out against the red sky in a new way
each evening, a certain stretch of wall eaten away by
light or shadow, a certain group of windows or tiles lit up.

I'd start out by walking along the first wall, crossing
fields and orchards; then, when I had my fill of the over-
hangs, I'd go off some distance, and in the same way that
I used the movable loopholes in the parapet walk I would
use the views from the village streets to compose the
"modes" of the castle, to sample sections of the surrounding countryside.

Alchemical is the word for those strolls of mine, colored by my readings in the huge library

—at the ninth of the twelve keys accompanying the
Exercises:

Jupiter with his scepter performs the function of Marshall, and in his honor Rhetoric raises an ashen sign on which Hope is painted, very ornately embellished with magnificent colors—

and my mineralogical daydreams

(the small spheres of oolitic kliachites, seeds to be sown in the clay fields the same color as harvests of aluminum;

asbestos serpentines the long fibers of which the Ancients wove into napkins that they bleached white by tossing into fire;

prisms of black tourmaline that would be cut up into thin strips for polarizing light . . .),

every sort of soil seemed to me capable of being cooked, every sort of grass swollen with precious saps, every reptile carrying potent venoms, every rock had to be concealing fissures that some sort of Open Sesame could part, every torrent rolling along nuggets, if not of gold—what did I care about gold?—but more generous substances

(pink hematite oligist, Ceylonese jargoons . . .),

suitable for fostering, in the simplest athanors, the distillation of the elixirs of immortality.

In these hillsides there was supposedly a series of caves that connected with our towers and the oldest convents in the region;

hyacinth quartzes of Compostello, pink rubellites, asparagus stones, translucid idiocrastes must have been nearing perfection, their mutations ongoing, the most ancient beasts still asleep inside, in age-old hibernation, within enormous globes guarded by abbots with beards and hair white as snow, keeping watch over their gently blazing furnaces for the birth of women of gold.

Dedaluses in hooded robes, amid their pentacles, their mirrors misting over at the slightest call from one of their brothers, or bleeding if some misfortune had occurred, for centuries they had been preparing long, swan-feathered wings

(deep in the Mediterranean, in the light of countless

flying sparks, around volcanic islands gushing with swarms of flickering embers

—banks of olivines and pyropes with pockets of scepter-shaped quartz haunted by dendrites—

they raised whole herds, their golems went down to feed them grain cooked with metal shavings and dew-soaked bread),

and if I succeeded in coming upon them by surprise, if I spoke the word they were expecting

(what libertine angel or what generous demon will be able to whisper it to me?),

a signal agreed upon in a very ancient past, patiently deciphered from one of those books of black magic spells on some winter night of the last century in the huge library, in some castle or abbey where it remained ever since, long before the installation of any alarms, modern MARANATHA,

they would fit them to my shoulders, sending down their sinewy roots into my shoulder blades by massaging them for a long time with a hot purple unguent,

and before they realized their mistake, I would soar off above the ripening crops and villages, then, when I became cold, I would fly back down laughing into their den, confessing my real status as a French student on vacation at the count's, I'd give them back their wings, slip into my modern suit and jacket, and, as the price of my silence, I would in turn make them sign a pact assuring my safety and my right to participate in their secrets.

Sunny, warm, the smell of hay . . .

Now in my sky there appears the immense abode with 365 windows plus a skylight,

baroque, stables in an arc with a sumptuous oval room in the center, painted with a fresco, for keeping saddles, a tiny chapel at the end of one wing, certainly installed with delightful organs, Mercury at the top of the center pavilion, brandishing his caduceus, inside a

white fabulously rich staircase with chubby cherubs
holding lanterns,

where one Friday I joined the count who had been
invited by the squire, heir to the sumptuous archbishop
prince, the man behind all this construction,

in order to be able to discuss with the librarian abbey a
few issues related to book conservation.

Since he had already been here, the count, before going up to the noble floor, gave me a tour of the grottoes.

A few steps lead down toward a porchway which, just
below the first landing, is crowned by a bearded face with
horns, at once terrifying and meekly mild, the guardian
of an underground world decorated with eight stucco
statues, larger than life:

the water sheathed in algae, spring wreathed with daf-
fodils,

surmounted by bas-reliefs:

Aquarius, Pisces, Aries

(the peasants quaff their wine, fish for trout, lead their
animals to pasture)

amid the flowing fountains

—the proportions are calculated to provide for maxi-
mum resonance—

under the ceiling paintings:

Asia with her elephants and tigers, Africa her lions
and giraffes.

And you walk into a small cubical room, on the left,
entirely painted in order to give the impression that it's
crumbling down

—sort of like that room of the Palazzo del Te in
Mantua, where Giulio Romano depicted the victory of the
gods over the Titans hurled to earth,

—the archbishop prince himself appearing in the role
of Samson shaking the columns of the Temple of Dagon,
thus commemorating through his painting his willful de-
struction of the castle of his fathers so that he could
build this one in its place.

The stucco appearance, a young woman sheathed in feathers, summer, a young man larger than life, wreathed in strawberries and blueberries,
Taurus, Gemini
(the peasants dance around a maypole, light a midsummer's night bonfire, sleep under the trees, take in the harvest)
Cancer, Leo in bas-relief,
amid the crystal incrustations:
sunflowers, steel gray mispickels,
—we've returned to the underground world—
rod-shaped natrolites, dawn red realgars, garnets from Bohemia, kunzites,
under the center divided into four sections:
morning welcomed by her roosters
—the French windows look out onto verdant Elysian fields where deer are grazing—
midnight caressed by her parakeets,
—under large trees tingeing the light of the deep ponds—
evening enchanted by her nightingales,
—the softest footfall sets off an endless echo—
night haunted by her birds of prey,
amid the incrusted seashells:
Venus's-combs, carpet-shell clams, giant clams, murices,
—between the two vast fireplaces used for warmth during holidays—
oysters, porcelains,
surrounding Virgo and Libra in bas-relief
(the peasants harvest grapes, shake down nuts; go hunting, pluck their geese)
Scorpio and Sagittarius,
above autumn in stucco, a handsome hairy man wreathed in vine branches, and fire, a woman larger than life, girdled in rays of light and flame.
And you walk into another small cubical room, on the

right, given over entirely to a landscape in ruins, Germany identified with a Roman countryside: Colosseum, aqueducts, dilapidated baths, contemplated with dreamy melancholy by the dark dog, the archbishop prince's favorite, fur bristling.

Under the paintings, curving along the ceiling of the underground world around the hours:

America with her elks and buffalo, Europe her wild boars and wolves,

amid the incrusted iridescent labradorite, staurolites in Brittany crosslets, violet fluorspar,

—reflected by the brass globes of two big chandeliers hanging by their chains—

ilmenites, jades,

(the peasants warm themselves by their fire)

Capricorn in bas-relief,

above the old earth sheathed in ferns and Old Man Winter wreathed in hoarfrost and snowflakes.

We climbed the white marble steps, deciphering on the ceiling of the immense cage, amid countless painted figures, a German inscription in beautiful and very neat colored Latin letters warning us:

As Phoebus lights the world, so Virtue is the adornment of men in the four corners of the world,

while turning, along with our gazes, around the caissons of the lower and upper galleries, the twelve labors of Hercules and the loves of Jupiter.

The abbot, librarian and bursar, on the small side, loquacious, in clergyman's garb, welcomes us into the vast polychrome salon where he had come to await us

(he spoke only German),

showed us across the large gallery, explaining to me:

"The majority of the paintings date from the end of the seventeenth century because the archbishop prince, after having once been interested in older artists, and discovering that the majority of the paintings that had been

sold to him were fakes, had decided to buy only from living painters."

We passed in front of the tulips of springtime, roses,
asters, snowdrops

"Here is the flower room, and the salon of the landscape in ruins"

(baths and Colosseum, but hadn't a painter taken it
upon himself to depict in ruins the very castle where we
were standing?),

quickly,

(Prudence in an azure veil, carrying a shield, Strength
draped in red, clutching a sword, pearly white Temperance admiring the refractions of a flask of pure water,
versicolored Hope, body wrapped around an anchor)

"the room of vices and virtues, the one of saints, male
and female"

(Paul in a white citrine robe edged in gold, holding an
unsheathed glaive, Peter in a citrine red, holding a key),

quickly, quickly,

(Joseph and Potiphar's wife, Joseph and the great cupbearer in their prison, Joseph interprets Pharaoh's
dreams)

"the room of Biblical events, the one of marine life"

(streams of oysters or Venus's-combs) . . .

the sound of voices.

As soon as we had greeted her, the countess heiress,
Italian-born, thickly powdered

(people whispered that she couldn't refuse her chap-
lain anything),

rose to show us along with all the other guests into the
dining room decorated with large still lifes by Jordaens
and Snyders under which had been arranged Dresden
china echoing the fruits, vegetables, or animals depicted
above.

From time to time I steal a glance at the park. The
deer. I think I'm dreaming. I'm startled; someone has
just asked me a question. I'm passed dishes, salt, a finger

bowl. This one person is talking about coins; he invites me to come for a visit if I'm ever passing through Munich.

I'm standing. I'm offered sugar, some kind of liquor.

Doors are closed behind us, the perky abbot takes us across the hunting room:

"We have lots of time now, you can linger over these lions, these tigers, these elk, these wolves, all this is the work of some students of Rubens, naturally; here is your castle, my dear fellow, and the prince's."

The gallery of German landscapes, the salon of the gods of Olympus:

"You can recognize Diana with her bow and her crescent moon, Mars with his helmet, Mercury with his wings and caduceus, but here's something more curious, this flight of a bull, an eagle, a swan and a shower of gold, that's Jupiter in a few of his lover's metamorphoses, you have the complete array in the caissons of the upper gallery of the monumental staircase. And here, some further metamorphoses: whereas Jupiter changes his shape for his own pleasure, these unfortunate creatures you see are all transformed by some god taking vengeance or punishing them. Acteon is changed into a stag, for example,"

the room of Ovid's *Metamorphoses,* the portrait gallery.

"An alchemist said to have lived in the fifteenth century, no need to tell you that the face is a pure fabrication; what this unknown man is holding in his hand is not a feather pen but an awl; this Jesuit is Father Kircher; ah! so amusing, aren't they, these dear little architects, these painters, the man who dangled by his tail end in order to daub the sky of his landscape, these sculptors—a metamorphosis about which the gods of Olympus, apparently, had never dreamed—these musicians, astronomers, alchemists and these extraordinary dear little writers,"

the ape room, the room of church interiors,
"We need to walk upstairs now."
The library under the rafters, much smaller than
H—'s, had the advantage over his of boasting precisely
those precious works which the princes von O— W— had
sold when their estates changed hands,
at times, no doubt, the very exact copies,
originals of Rousseau, Diderot, Voltaire, Sade,
Mundus Subterraneus and *China Illustrated* by Father Kircher,
The Butterflies of Surinam,
along with some splendid Ottoman and Abassid manuscripts.
Since the abbot and the count had stepped off into a
window nook, talking in hushed tones about the difficulties of their relationship with certain universities,
—a bell somewhere—
having spotted on an oval table a small, severely damaged work that I seemed to recognize, I couldn't resist
the pleasure of opening and reading it
(thinking I was dreaming):
. . . when it was the fifth night . . .

(I was imagining the moon)

. . . So they rested that night in mutual embrace Dunyazad . . .

(and on her bare ankles sticking out of the blankets
she wore rings of droplet topaz)

. . . awoke at the usual time and called the Sultan Shahryar . . .

(on her bare breasts over which was spread his long
black beard, a necklace of red cobalt flowers)

. . . speaking up I would wish said he to hear the story of that
ape I'm going to satisfy your curiosity Sire answered Sharazad . . .

(on her bare arms, galena bracelets)

. . . the Sultan continued the second Kalandar son of the King
while still addressing Zobeide . . .

(a diadem formed from leaves of iridescent hematite)

... paid no attention to the other writings ...

I saw a shadow moving across the beach, the count poked fun at me.

The abbot, growing worried, or so it seemed to me, showed us back down in silence through the room of Dutch interiors, the smaller rooms of proverbs and of *Jerusalem Delivered,* the salons of the martyrs and the liberal arts, the gallery of the overseas landscapes,

the salon of mirrors, all in marquetry and mirrors, mirrored ceiling, with all the porcelains which a boat especially chartered by the archbishop prince had been able to bring back from Japan and China,

and walked us over to the bus.

While saying our good-byes, a nightingale's song.

Then the ripe fields flashed past under the shepherd's star, the bunches of grapes, the ferns, the earth sheathed in its last flames,

while we drove toward our needle peaks of uranophane, disthenes of the Ticino, epidotes, the views of the obelisks in Rome by Piranese and the ancient maps of Surinam in the Knights' Chamber, the shelves of books on rhetoric, the voyages in the cell in the company of the archangel Uriel as far as the bronzed plains of Jupiter with stumps of cassiterite,

toward Basil Valentine saying to Jacob Böhme across (perhaps) the centuries:

When noble Venus assumes government, and, following custom, justly distributes the duties of the royal court, she appears in great splendor, and for her Music presents a magnificent red banner on which is painted Charity, very beautiful in green vestments,

and in *The Art of Finding Happiness Through Dreams,* those recipes, made of various bases, of chrysocolla, amanita, or vanessa, to find in the night a woman you've loved and lost.

One evening, and for a certain number after that, along the river W—, watching for the towers to appear between the oak branches and the rock spurs,

studying the barks, vervures, mosses, gravel, strata,

rocks that were commoners like me: granites, clays, gneiss, chalks, coal, flint, marbles.

Every so often an automobile passed, a bicycle a little more frequently, a horse-drawn cart; on the other bank, I could make out the former synagogue, spared because it had been converted into a barn ages ago.

On my way back a very steep path led me to a small secret door in the first castle wall, which I walked through. When I turned the creaking ruby knob, the towers were still able to shine above their countryside, a few tatters of twilight clinging to the roof tiles, a few crimson feathers of clouds crossing the sky, I knew that the grass in the courtyard, the trees, the parapet walk would sink deeper every time in their lake of night, that the enormous library, the church and its bell tower, the bakery and its tower, the torture chamber tower, the tower of mineralogy and Bavarian armor would turn into greenish black masses like chunks of coal covered in algae; in the witch's house, the guard tower and that of the apartments, a few lights.

After total darkness had fallen, in order to win at The Castle of the Carpathians, the count constructed a tower: foundations (tens), crypt and vault (eights), chapel, stone paving (sixes), salon, ceiling (fours) fitting into the "optical device," terrace (twos), and the crenels (aces).

I was reading the book about the castle of H—.

At a certain distance away on the table, the count built the inn of King Mathias (floor tiling, roof tiles with spades, pierced shutters with clubs and hearts), guarded by his vassal Alexander who was wrapped in discussion with the forester Nic Deck.

I always found myself returning to the chapter on executions.

Once Baron Rodolphe-David de Gortz was installed in his salon, Nic Deck-Lancelot attempted to scale the disturbing village, while Miriota, his Cleopatra, waited for him back at the inn.

July 24, 1667: Margaretha Ruder of Leiheim, for infanticide, caned, banished;
August 2, 1667: Georg Otter heretofore intendant of the O— at Forheim, for blasphemy, caned, banished . . .

In the chapel, the inventor César Orfanik, by means of mechanisms and machinations, foiled the daring man, and the two lovers, Nic Deck and Miriota, wound up broken-hearted back in front of the inn, whose room was now free for Count Franz of Télek, whose valet slept in the attic.

I closed the book, looked at the cards, the count explained to me:

"Orfanik makes La Stilla appear in the 'optical device' at the very moment when she's singing, during her farewell festival at the San Carlo in Naples, the aria from *Orlando:*

Inamorata, mio cuore tremante,
Voglio morire . . .

and upon the Italian words of Jules Verne the count made up a Handelian melody that he murmured in his falsetto.

The voice of the queen of hearts brought the young Franz-Charles of Télek out of the inn of King Mathias, while a little farther away on the table, in the village of Karlsburg, two men-at-arms were climbing into bed with their wives.

The lamp kindled a spark from the flask over the fireplace.

Franz of Télek, having made it inside the castle, found himself shut in the crypt. Rotzko-Lahire was going to wake up the men-at-arms whose terrorized wives took refuge in the inn. Orfanik went up to the top of one of the crenels, the king of hearts went to the chapel, his valet entered the crypt.

Silence had fallen again, briefly broken by the sound of cards in play. I picked up my book once more; I tried to become interested in the former Princess von O— W—. I leafed through the pages.

After David, Stilla's apparition fled across one of the crenels; frantic young Charlemagne pursued her right into the "optical device."

Once again I fell into the trap:

1673: Katharina Engellender of Dürrenzimmern, for infanticide, banished *in perpetuum;* Hans Georg Struber of Bavaria, *idem* for theft,

March 18, 1676: Walpurga Schweickardt of Schopfloch, for having with premeditation pushed her son-in-law into the fountain and drowned him, executed by sword . . .

Franz of Télek arrived on the last crenel, followed by four valets. A bell somewhere tolled in C—. Then the castle exploded, all the debris reforming in the shape of a porchway inside of which the wedding procession marched:

first, the three corpses of the baron, of the inventor and of the soprano, then Franz of Télek gone mad, supported by the soldier Rotzko, the two men-at-arms with their wives, the innkeeper, and finally the newlyweds in their garments embroidered with spades.

After the count had retired, one night, unable to resist another moment, and doing my best not to make the slightest sound (the old parquet floor under my bare feet), I went up to the fireplace, took hold of the flask, opened it, took a long whiff—some sort of wine—and recorked it.

10

Games of Solitaire

The porters came back to the ship, and stated their order
to the captain. He answered that it was a matter for the
rector. They immediately wrapped me in a toga of the university colors, violet and blue, and carried me in their
arms across the dock right into a sumptuous open car-
riage.

The port, the streets, the squares, the windows, all were
filled with a multitude of students of both sexes and all
ages, drawn by curiosity from all corners of the city, for
the rumor had spread just now that the rector had chosen
an ape as his secretary.

I found that with his beard and hair white as snow,
dressed in purple from head to foot, he looked like Jupiter
sitting among the eleven other officials. After bowing
deeply to him three times, I remained on my backside,
head bowed, in ape posture.

On the organ a trill in fourth played with idocrase
technique.

The whole assembly admired me to no end, unable to
understand how it was possible for an ape to know how to
render to rectors the respect due them, and he himself,
eyes moon white, was the most astonished.

Once the ceremony ended, there remained by his side
only the dean of the School of Writing, very elderly, a

small and very young North African streetsweeper, and myself. He sat down to wait, motioned me over to share his meal, an enigmatic look in his eyes.

First, the reading of a few lines I had written out on a huge peach, in the hand of Basil Valentine, in gratitude, before the dishes were cleared away, then, after leaving the table, on the cup he had presented to me as he was being brought his Tokay, the lines I had inscribed in the hand of Jacob Böhme, in order to explain how I came to find myself in such a state after so much hardship, increased his astonishment, and His Magnificence, having ordered a deck of cards to be brought, asked me by motioning with his eyes white as the moon's clubs, whether I knew how to win at solitaire, and wanted me to compete against him.

Kissing the violet and blue carpet on which were depicted Judith and Cleopatra in orange dresses, and carrying my forehands on my head, I indicated that I was ready to receive this honor.

He played a hand of the Almanach de Gotha (ten of alum, nine of ciocoite against an ermine background), and I countered with How to Succeed (seven of epidote, eight of galena on a bed of dirt);

he came back with Witch Hunt (six of ilmenite, five of kunzite against a leaf of parchment), to which I retorted with Joseph in Egypt (three of mispickel, four of olivine against a sandy desert);

he then delivered The Castle of the Carpathians (two of quartz, ace of serpentine on a snowy sky), but The 1001 Nights made victory mine,

and noticing in his orange eyes that this saddened him somewhat, by way of consolation I composed, in the hand of Father Kircher, a few lines in which I told him that two powerful disputers had waged a very caustic argument the whole day long, but by evening they had reached a mutual accord, and spent a very agreeable night together in the same room where they had debated.

So many things struck the rector as being so far beyond anything he had ever seen or heard with regard to the skill and intelligence of apes, he didn't wish to be the sole witness of these amazing feats:

"Go," he said, his eyes gold, to the dean of the School of Writing, who in the past had possessed a special interest in the education of his daughter, the beautiful student, "have your pupil come here, I would be greatly pleased for her to share in my delight."

The dean hastened off to find Eva Erber, who crossed the threshold while striking delightful music from a zither slung around her neck. She had just taken her shower, and only a moment before had slipped into the sleeves of her green dressing gown, but as soon as she stepped into the room, she pulled it closed over her legs and her splendid bosom, crying out:

"Most illustrious one, Your Magnificence must have forgotten. I am very surprised that you have had me come before these gentlemen dressed the way I am."

On the organ a trill in a silky fifth played with kieselguhr technique.

"What do you mean, daughter of mine," the rector answered, "the only people here are the small North African sweeper, who is still too young to have thoughts of women, the dean of the School of Writing, your instructor, who has never disturbed you, and myself! Yet you close your peignoir up to your neck and you make such ado . . ."

"Most illustrious one," the student replied, her eyes white and black, "Your Magnificence is going to discover that I am not mistaken. The ape you see is in reality the young student Férenc de Télek, pupil and rival of the professor baron of Gortz. He was transformed into an ape by evil design. The vampire Orfanik, son of the daughter of Nosferatu, is responsible for this malicious turn, after having cruelly taken the life of Stilla, soprano of the theater of San Carlo in Naples, daughter of the rector of the University of the Fulcanelli Figures."

She spoke a refined Hungarian, fluent, old-fashioned, exquisite, with a certain languid, graceful ease in the consonants, and to my great stupefaction, I understood her perfectly, I was able to perceive the least of her lilting intonations.

The rector, surprised by this speech, turning toward me, and not motioning to me in signs anymore, asked me whether his daughter spoke the truth. I motioned in the negative, but he interpreted my gestures to mean the opposite.

"My daughter," he continued, and he nervously leafed through a copy of Aristotle, "how do you know that this Hungarian student was transformed into an ape by evil design?"

"Most illustrious one," the student answered, and she dreamily leafed through a score by Ockegem, "Your Magnificence will remember that toward the end of my childhood I had an old assistant for a tutor. She was a very clever vampirologist: she taught me the seven times seven rules of her science, by virtue of which I would be able, in the wink of an eye, to transport your university to coral atolls and reefs of coppery shells, glory of the oceans of Venus. At first glance I ascertained the identity of this transformed person and the culprit behind his misfortune."

"My daughter," the rector said, "I didn't imagine you to be so clever."

"Most illustrious one," the student answered, her eyes gold and orange, "while such curious things are well worth knowing, I felt that I should not boast of them."

"Might you then be able to reverse the student's transformation?" . . .

11

☉rbits

Tons of clouds.

The author of *The Signature of Things* responded to that of *The Triumphal Chariot of Antimony:*

An oil sweeter than any sugar . . .

I no longer know in which order I managed to visit those reserves of ages past; in memory they form a wreathlike ring of planets circling their star, which is H—. So then, ignoring the precise sequence in which they rose above the horizon of my stay, I hop from sphere to sphere, and here I am arriving not only in the count's company, but especially with my guardian angel Athanasius "Uriel" Kircher, in another small castle whose initial I've forgotten. What remains with me are only images at dusk—of hay wagons returning to nearby granges, crimson arbors, pink and brown bricks.

Trouts of algae of clouds.

In the following days I again found our milky pink feldspars, our variscites in veined rognons, *The Rake's Progress* by Hogarth, and very old maps of the New Indies in the Knights' Chamber, Jacob Böhme:

It contains all the pearls in the world, the most freshly flowing waters . . .

Herds of clouds.

Inside, cigar smoke, tapestries, and a Louis XVI clock whose pendulum was a swing with a shepherdess carrying a basket, which rocks to and from the viewer.

An evening of linguistic obscurity, only German was spoken, and I caught just a word here and there, but with each discovery I was so proud, I smiled, smiled, I just couldn't stop smiling.

Swinging flowers of clouds.

This is where Lady Venus hides her jewel box; she's the Virgin with her small crown . . .

The shelves on dialectics, in *The Art of Finding Happiness Through Dreams,* the recipes made of various bases, galence, snapdragon, or hair of wolf in order to overpower your enemy in your dreams, in the book on the castle of H—:

May 10, 1676: Michael Steinbeck, young soldier, native of Wiener Neustat, age thirteen, for sodomy, executed by sword . . .

The shelves of geometry, and going back to the *Mysterium Magnum:*

Earth dweller, if only you could still have it! Lucifer and Adam have lost it for us, Man, if only you knew what was hidden there, what desire! But such appears only to the elect. O noble pearl, how smooth you are in your new birth, what brilliance! . . .

Torches of feathers of Venus's-combs of clouds.

An islet of French in this German lake:

"And you, monsieur, what brings you to this country?"

"I've come to admire."

Ever since, in each castle, I was welcomed by the reputation which this response had earned for me.

The following days:

In this point, O philosophers, resides the strength and action of your precious stones, of your tincture which quickens the pale waters of the Moon; for here Jupiter is prince, and the Sun, king, and Lady Venus, the gentlest spouse of the king. But beforehand, Mars/Lucifer ought to set down his scepter, Christ bind him in

chains and enliven with his oil of heavenly blood the poor sullied
Moon, so that anger can be transmuted into delight. It is in this
way that the Great Art is born . . .

The rotunda at the summit of the Prince's tower
—a bell—
with the badly damaged small volume on the oval
table:

. . . continued Shahrazad . . .

(fresh as water)

. . . I must remain here my sister said Dunyazad . . .

(invigorating as air)

. . . now there's a very wondrous tale . . .

Reveries of fêtes galantes, scenes from the life of a
good-for-nothing.
Shadows of landslides of orchards of porcelains of
clouds.
Calcites shaped like nail heads, crocoites, chromifer-
ous diopsides, fluorescent and translucid willemites, the
rotunda:

. . . you are not wrong responded the Sultana . . .

(voluble as night)

. . . and if the Sultan . . .

(calm as earth)

. . . if this pious and auspicious King permit me . . .

Jacob Böhme:

The seventh day, Saturday, Saturn . . .

Ripe fields of ruins of flames of murices of clouds.
Once I went with the count's children to visit their
former teacher, a French woman, who had taken up per-
manent residence with the family through marriage with

the forester. The household staff had joined the masters in their flight and their new living arrangements. Prince von O— W— had found a place in his forests.

A small house out of a German fairy tale. I was, I thought, the first Frenchman this woman had seen since before the war. Stands of tall trees, I strolled around as if in an organ.

Ripe grapes of bunches of oysters of clouds.

Moses said that, when God made man, he planted a garden in Eden . . .

The shelves of arithmetic, a bell somewhere, the list of executions:

July 15, 1676: Georg Müller, former payment officer at Magerbein, but native of Pfäfflingen, executed by rope; a "brother of Jacob," Michaël Rüpel and his wife, for having uttered threats for several weeks in a row, taken into custody and driven from the country . . .

The Disasters of War by Jacques Callot and very old maps of German cities in the Knights' Chamber, turning back to the chapter on Paradise:

The world of gloom revealed in the sacred world of light and the latter in the outer world which was its manifestation . . .

The shelves of rhetoric and music.

Foliage of ferns of clouds.

To this first ring of castles and villages, there was soon added another, of cities: Augsburg, Nuremberg.

And the outer world reveled in the two inner worlds which were its life; and there existed between them a noble benevolence, a mutual liking . . .

Leaving the two children in the foresters' care, we took the train, one Saturday, the count, the countess, and I

(a splinter went into my right eye),

and we went to spend a week in a charming Munich villa lent to them by friends, no doubt also refugees from some castle of the Sudetenland, and naturally the memory of Jacob Böhm followed me there:

Man's strength was so powerful before vanity . . .

after strolling along the absinth-colored river, amid
the royal parks, the zoo with its ape collection, and the
galleries,
the haunting obsession with executions:

April 28, 1677: Anna Reussner of Mauren, for infanticide, executed by sword, her head displayed to the court . . .

in the evening, while the count, who had brought his
deck of cards, explained to me in the salon, before I went
back to my self-contained garret room, how to win at The
1001 Nights,
first setting down a guard of nine spades (from the two
to the ten), a paving floor of diamonds, a carpet of nine
clubs and a mattress of hearts,
on which he stretched a Charlemagne Shahryar surrounded by Scheherazade and Dunyazade menaced by
the ace of spades and offered hope by the ace of clubs

. . . at the end of the sixth night Dunyazad . . .

(fresh as morning)

. . . pleaded the Sultana . . .

(quivering as spring)

. . . to tell the rest of this wondrous tale that she was unable to
finish the night before readily answered Shahrazad . . .

(voluptuous as the New Indies)

. . . Thereupon the second Kalandar came forward; and, kissing
the ground, began to tell . . .

arranging above the bed, in the sky of the tale, the
king of clubs who was changed into an ape valet in a second sky higher up
(furs of clouds)

. . . continuing to tell his story to Zobeide . . .

taking Scheherazade herself and placing her in the
sky of the stories
(ganders of hoarfrosts of clouds),

. . . has two sisters . . .

Judith-Amine, Saphie-Cleopatra,

. . . to the two other Kalandars . . .

David and Caesar,

. . . to the Caliph . . .

Shahryar himself in the sky of the stories
(embers of clouds),

. . . to the Wazir Giafar to the Eunuch Mesrour and to the Porter . . .

Hector, Ogier, Lahire,

. . . declared the Princess Lady of Beauty . . .

moving up Pinarzade to the second sky of the stories,

. . . hending in hand an iron knife whereon was inscribed in He-
brew characters . . .

(I was reading *The Other Side* by Alfred Kubin, which
a friend of the count had lent me, Monsieur Noir, reader
at the main theater, whose ambition was to assemble in
his tiny room a sample of each century for each nation)

. . . she had us next bring down the Sultan . . .

Harun al-Rashid,

. . . the Chief of the eunuchs . . .

Mesrour,

. . . the young slave . . .

the Porter,

. . . and I in a secret courtyard of the palace . . .

which was possible only before the sun appeared, the ace of diamonds, for at that point the tale broke off, we had to wait until the next night, bring back the King of Persia, the sultana and his sister in the huge bed, start the story over again

. . . and described a wide circle in the midst of the palace hall, and therein wrote in Cufic letters, called Cleopatra characters . . .

(in order to decipher them I applied the principles of the *Œdipus Ægyptiacus* and I then recognized the maxim by Jacob Böhme:

The seventh day is the origin and the beginning of the first . . .),

unless before the sun rises the ace of hearts has managed to replace the spade above the head of Scheherazade, in which case, in the sky of the stories, the Kalandars could then marry Zobeide's sisters.

12

The Tournament

Margaretha Rüder of Leiheim finished readying a device, very beautiful in her tightly belted green dressing gown whose collar remained loose enough to allow me a glimpse of her marvelous breasts. Then, her eyes white and black, she took up her place at the control panel where she proceeded to adjust the settings.

Imperceptibly the air grew so dark it seemed night had fallen and that the machine of the world was going to dissolve.

We grew extremely frightened at the appearance of Michael Weckhle, son of the daughter of Nosferatu, in the shape of a dog with green eyes ringed with circles alternately Saturn white and citrine white.

"Monster, instead of crawling before me, you dare appear in this horrible guise!"

"You're going to pay for the trouble you've put me through to come here!"

He opened a horrifying maw and moved in her direction to devour her.

But Katharina Engelländer of Dürrenzimmern aimed the device called a "lead trumpet," with lamps of lamellar zeolite, whose construction was based on a description in a sole surviving copy of Mundus Subigneus between silver covers, which sliced the dog in two.

On the organ a trill in a resinous sixth played with moroxite technique.

His head changed into a large wild boar; the other half disappeared.

The student, extinguishing her trumpet on the spot, her eyes gold and orange, aimed at him a "lead dog" with willemite fangs, such as is drawn in the Africa Illustrata, and waged such a hard-fought battle with Thomas Reinisch that he flew off, a vulture with orange eyes, circles Moon white and Mars black.

Walpurga Schweickardt of Schopfloch took off in pursuit, through the skylight, a "lead wild boar" with variscite tusks, described in a Mundus Subigneus between iron covers encrusted with cinnabar and tin. We watched as he disappeared from sight into the clouds.

The floor tiles parted; Martin Stumpflein emerged, a hare with bristling fur, yelping in a horrifying way. A "lead vulture" with beak of uranophane, such as is drawn in the America Illustrata, burst onto the scene and swooped upon him.

The hare, changing into a worm next to The Book of Figures, instantly bored through the copper cover and hid inside.

The volume then swelled, became as large as The Butterflies of Surinam, rising to the laboratory roof from where, after having circled on itself several times while fluttering its pages, it dropped amid the instruments, shredding itself into pieces spotted with ocellus, blue centers ringed with halos alternately citrine white and gold.

After extinguishing the vulture, the student with the planetary earrings had set into motion a "lead hare" with topaz claws, which pounced on the supple bark, munching it like grass.

But, at the very moment he was about to gobble down the last remaining leaf, he slipped on the staurolite coping and was transformed into an ichthyosaurus.

Quickly throwing off her green dressing gown, Anna Reussner of Mauren chased it underwater for seven whole hours. Jacob Strauss of Reimlingen (unless it was Lorenz Burger, nicknamed the Ferryman) and we quivered, not knowing what had become of them, seeing horrible black bubbles ringed with waves alternately orange and azure.

On the organ a trill in a muddy sixth played with onyx technique.

Wearing a solid citrine red uniform, with a large coat on which was embroidered the face of Caesar, holding a lightning bolt in his right hand, and resting his left on the shoulder of Judith, kneeling at his feet, in an orange dress, holding a scroll on which was written in beautiful and very neat letters of realgar:

Vampire precor est crudelis,

Veit Höckinger of Bavaria and the completely naked student, luminescent, breathing sparks, slowly rose from the foam toward each other until they started grappling.

Suddenly breaking free, Michael Rüpel, his body incandescent (unless it was Georg Müller), spewing swirls of thick and fiery smoke, was already drawing near the corner where we were trembling, and despite her great dispatch, Margaretha Hausbrändl of Ebermergen could not prevent the blue-eyed rector's beard from going up in flames, the dean of the School of Writing from choking to death, a splinter from blinding me in one eye . . .

Yet abruptly the student appeared in all her natural splendor, nervously refastening the belt of her green dressing gown, and Michael Steinbeck of Weiner Neustadt, thirteen years old, found himself reduced to a heap of ashes . . .

13

The German Museum

I'd rubbed my eyes when I woke up in the celebrated capital of the mad kings where the large museum of natural sciences and technology was awaiting me:

the earth, the earth's crust, the diorama of the Grand Canyon . . .,

which haunted me amid the paintings of the art gallery in ruins, in those days exhibited in the Nazi "Haus der Kunzt":

the underground world, rocks, the growth of life . . .,

as I was visiting an enormous art exhibition on the High Middle Ages dating from the paleo-Christian era to early Gothic, in the palace of Prince Charles, where there were in particular Irish manuscripts and the Romanesque Christ in ivory from the Bamberg cathedral:

formation of deposits, rock salt, naphtha . . .,

as I was attending, in a temporary room ingeniously set up in the ruins of the Opéra, *The Tragical History of Doctor Faust* directed and acted by Orson Welles, with music by Duke Ellington:

seismographs, soundings, signpostings for mineshafts . . .

and on my way back amid the bohemites, the alums in octahedral chains, the bluish beryls in their small cardboard compartments:

oratory of an old mine in the Mining Hills, construction of shafts, transportation and extraction facilities . . .,

as I was leafing through one last time the plates of the *Apocalypsis cum Figuris* by Albert Dürer and ancient star maps in the Knights' Chamber, Perseus always imperturbably rescuing Andromeda:

copies drawn from life of former metal, oil, and salt mines . . .,

as I came back to ponder, to examine one last time our Irish manuscript, our ivory Christ (I said "our")

mine lighting, ventilation, water pumping and safety facilities . . .,

as I was skimming one last time the shelves of dialectics, geometry, arithmetic

(a bell somewhere tolled in F),

as I was settling down in the cell in order to throw myself into the arms of the archangel Athanasius Uriel Kircher as far as the rings of Saturn

(the count walked by in the courtyard without his cane),

as I was listening to Basil Valentine who echoed Jacob Böhme:

Saturn is named Master of the court, when he fulfills his duties, Astronomy carries in his honor a black standard on which is painted Faith clothed in yellow and red

(the countess came back up from an errand in the village),

as I was amusing myself with my discoveries in *The Art of Finding Happiness Through Dreams* of recipes made of various bases, native gold, oak apple, or crow's blood, in order to learn your future

(the guard at the head of a band of tourists was twirling around his bunch of keys),

as I continued to toll, one by one, dumbfounded, in the annals of the castle, I couldn't stop myself, the knell of the capital executions:

August 9, 1677, for various thefts, executed by rope, December 23, for infanticide, executed by sword, 1678, for various crimes, executed by sword . . .

(the tourists passed along the parapet walk from the Mineralogy Tower to the Torture Chamber),

a knell that also haunted me, which I attempted to escape by climbing all the way to the rotunda one last time, there to read:

. . . if thou art an ape by ensorcellment . . .

(my eye started giving me trouble again),

the knell:

for murder, executed by sword, February 14, 1680, sodomite, executed by sword, then burned with his horse, March 30, previously a forester, succumbed in his prison cell . . .

(O memories of the museum of natural sciences and technology of the Bavarian capital, how reassuring you were!),

. . . such then is my story this is what caused the loss of my eye.—And Shahrazad perceived the dawn of day . . .

O beauty, protect me, beauty!
(an American bomber flew overhead)

. . . beginning over I must stop at this point . . .

(my eye kept hurting me more and more),

April 18, 1718: the "long man" and the Gypsy Leyenberger, commonly known as the Twisted Gypsy, hanged

—in the book of the executioner Johannes Michael Kober, the following points of information can be found:

December 15, 1717, I tortured the offender with thumbscrews and the boot, and I administered them on his wife—3 florins

(what play were the children staging at this hour with their curtains on the rising hill? *The Tragical History of Doctor Faust?*),

... I cannot admire my sister enough then said Dunyazad ...

O brightness, protect me!
(the wall-dwelling falcons screeching),

February 4, 1718, I administered on the "long man" and his wife tortured them—2 florins

(a gust of wind)

... the adventures which you've just recounted I know countless like them answered the Sultan ...

indefatigable
(a window banging),

February 15, I had to treat the "long man" so that the cut he gave himself in his neck would not be able to hinder matters, for two visits—2 florins

(I went over to shut it),

... which are even more wondrous Shahryar ...

O marvelous ear, completely intact amid the fury!
(the wind),

March 2, I stretched him out on the rack and gave him thirty lashes; since, according to the custom of this land, thirty kreutzers is paid per lash, there should be here added—4 florins

(the trees twisted by the wind),

... waiting to find out whether the end of the story of the second Kalandar would be as agreeable as its beginning put off until the next day the death of the Sultana.

O voices, O suspense!
(on the rising hill the children had disappeared),

March 10, I had, according to the order of his High Lordship, searched the so-called "long man" in order to check whether he was equipped with any *maleficium*—1 florin

(the dust of the cemetery blown back by the wind),
against the roving horror, protect me!
(darkening),

March 12, I had once again to administer the rack—1 florin

(the rain),
against these rumbles, against these grumbles, against these creaks, against these roars, against these cackles . . .
(the pounding on the windowpanes),

March 14, I once again tortured the "long man" and his wife—2 florins

(the banging on the roof tiles),
haunted me as I was skimming, that last Sunday, the shelves of rhetoric, of music, of astronomy,
gold letters on leather, ink letters on parchment
(faded sky),

June 2, 1681: Michael Weickhle, peasant of Niederroden, for sodomy, executed by rope upon a stake then burnt . . .

(the guard showed a last group of tourists up to the door of the last wolf),
as I was setting down one last time in the cell in order to soar to the nearest star
(the guard was putting away the table and the benches of the refreshment stand),

October 29, 1681: Margaretha, daughter of the master mason Wolf Schwertberger of H—, executed by sword . . .

(the children of the count were playing Witch Hunt),
or heard Basil Valentine continuing:

The Sun is the ruler of the kingdom and Grammar precedes him with a yellow flag on which can be seen Justice in gold lamé

(night fell much earlier than on those first evenings),
executed by sword, executed by rope, executed by wheel, burnt . . .
(the guard's wife lit the stove),
and Jacob Böhme answered him:

In the depths stretching beyond the Moon . . .

(last sunlight on the tiles of a few stories),

. . . 1742: the murderer Jörg Michael Günzel tortured to death by sword . . .

(a light came on in a window of the witch's house),

There exists neither night nor morning nor evening . . .

(the clouds)

October 29, 1774: The infanticide Anna Maria Brenner of Mönchsdeggingen, executed by sword . . .

(lights came on in a few windows in the tower of the Knights' Chamber, at the count's, at his relatives'),

but a perpetual day stretching from the beginning to the end of the world . . .

(the green sky),
texts which also haunted me on my way down into the courtyard
(the countess was calling her children),

July 15, 1746: The thief Hans Michael Bleysteiner of Kronheim, executed by sword . . .

(the moon)
on my way up the stairway of the Rotten Tower
(a planet),

And if Adam had stood his test, men would have walked the earth naked . . .

(I let the children move along ahead of me),
as I was looking for the last time at the count playing The Wheel of the Planets after dinner in the salon that served as my bedroom
(a bell),

April 18, 1749: Thomas Schaffler, blacksmith in Diemantstein, and his sister-in-law Magdalena Müller, for *incestus et adulterii saepius reiterati,* executed by sword . . .

(total darkness),

separating first the light from the shadows, he laid
down an earth of diamonds, barren and empty
(on the fireplace mantel, the flask),

for in paradise the celestial interpenetrated the outer world and
was its garment . . .

(on the small bookcase where the issues of the *Almanach de Gotha* sat in a row, I'd placed the book on the
castle of H—),
and make appear above the horizon the king of diamonds, the future sun
(clouds across the moon)

June 12, 1750: The grocer Joseph Spänkuh of Ellwangen, for
robbery and murder, executed by wheel, his wife freed from prison,
his sister-in-law Margaretha Schönnmann banished . . .

(all the other windows of the castle were dark),
separating the lower waters from the upper, spades,
on each side of the earth, constituting an ocean and a firmament
(I was holding in my hand the *Guide to the Museum of
Natural Sciences and Technology,* called the German
Museum, which I had brought back from Munich:)
—gnomons, astrolabes, sextants . . .
(everybody was asleep in the castle except for us two),
and making appear above the horizon the queen of diamonds Moon
(the two cupids molded in stucco on the ceiling),

and he would go in great beauty, joy and delight, his head child-
like . . .

(my suitcase was ready under the sofa, inside I had already packed *The Philosophic Abodes*),
growing grass, trees and plants of clubs on the earth's
surface
(a plane passed in the sky),
—artificial satellites, echo of the moon, planetari-
ums . . .

(my eye was burning)

and making appear above the horizon the jack of club Mars.

(the portrait of the count's brother, life-size, above my bed, with the iron cross, the snow . . .),

March 9, 1753: The coppersmith Franz Karl Rieder, native of Neuller near Ellwangen, executed by wheel for banditry and robberies; his wife Maria Josepha put in the stocks with her father-in-law Joseph Schmoll . . .

(there was a chill in the air),

arranging the stars, ace, upon the firmament beyond the planets

(I got up to close the window),

—far-off worlds, galaxies, chemistry of the stars . . .

(the odors of the damp courtyard),

and making appear above the horizon the jack of diamonds Mercury

(the two other windows were already closed),

The kingdom of the earth was their plaything, they would have had every metal for playthings until God would have transfigured the outer world: for them there would not have existed either dread, or fear, or any law for ordering or defending, for everything would have been permitted them. Adam would have been their great prince, and they would have lived in the world and yet also in the sky, in both worlds at once; paradise would have reigned throughout the universe . . .

(I came back toward the table),

begetting animals, hearts, on the earth amid the plants

(I tried reading where I left off, or rather re-examining a few illustrations in the guidebook:)

—alchemy laboratory, distillation, baroque pharmacy . . .

(the count offered me a small cigar),

and making appear above the horizon the king of hearts Jupiter

(lit it for me),

December 10, 1756: Hans Jörg Thum of Forheim, for murder of
his own master, executed by wheel . . .

(a cry very far off like the barking of a dog or the howl-
ing of a wolf),
setting out the man and woman, jack, queen of clubs,
amid the animals and plants of the Garden of Eden
(but the smoke was stinging my eyes far too much),
—crystallography, *lusus naturae,* chemical man . . .
(I tried hiding it with my right hand, but I quickly
gave up),
and making appear above the horizon the queen of
hearts Venus
(the door: the cigar butt kept smoking on its own in the
ashtray),
then taking a rest by making appear above the horizon
the king of clubs Saturn, his reign transmutable into a
golden age
(the shadow of the count's profile on the wall between
the two windows; the smoke rising, a very thin column
through the still air),
then turning over the first of the three remaining
cards
(the count's eye: I don't know what color it is),
if it was the demon (jack of spades), the game had to
be started all over
(the count's disappointment),
if it was the angel (jack of hearts), you had to pick up
all the planets, make a week pass in the world, once
again turn over the first of the three cards
(I shivered; "Fall's almost here," the count said; the
lamp's reflection in one of the windows),
if it was the tree (queen of spades), the man and
woman at last possessed knowledge
(leaning over a little I could see him in another window),
and the two jacks turned into Cain and Abel, both

delighting in paradise
(standing, like his brother in the painting),
even after he had retired to his bedroom, as I gave in
at last to the temptation to taste the contents of that
flask on the fireplace mantel,

May 22, 1761: Anton Storz, for commerce with the devil and
search for treasures, executed by sword . . .

sweet, fruity, with a smoky aftertaste, the product of a
smoke distillation, yes, maybe Tokay is just what it was.

14

Banishment

"The fire came inside me during that terrible battle, and I feel that it is consuming me little by little . . ."

On the organ a trill in a dull seventh played with quartz technique.

"My daughter," answered the treasure-hunter Anton Storz, his eyes silver blue, "you can see the state your father is in. Alas! I'm astonished that I'm still alive; Hans Jörg Thum of Forheim, your instructor, has died on the wheel, and the student you've just rescued from his transmutation has lost an eye."

Sighs and sobs cut off his words. While our own distress grew as though we were trying to outdo each other, Margaretha Schwertberger of H— started to shout:

"I'm burning, I'm burning!"

And stopped only after death had put an end to her unbearable pain. In a matter of moments she was completely reduced to ashes like Michael Steinbeck of Weiner Neustadt.

I would have preferred to spend my whole life as an ape or a dog than to see my benefactress die such a wretched death. For his part, the coppersmith Franz Karl Rieder of Neuller, near Ellwangen, his eyes azure iron, let out pitiful cries, then fainted.

Merchants and delivery men rushing over at his cries

had little trouble in bringing around the grocer Joseph Spänkuh of Ellwangen; no need to provide them with a lengthy account of this adventure in order to persuade them of the pain we felt, the names by which we called the two heaps of ashes allowed them to imagine easily enough.

His eyes orange mercury, with barely enough strength to support himself, the blacksmith Thomas Schaffer of Diemantstein leaned on his apprentices all the way back to his house.

As soon as the news of such a tragic event had spread throughout the quarter and the city, everyone had begun to pity the misfortune of the beautiful student and had joined in the affliction of the thief Michael Bleysteiner of Kronheim, his eyes black tin. For seven days every ceremony of deepest mourning: to the wind the ashes of Michael Steinbeck, those of the student collected in a gold crucible in order to mature in a mausoleum of idocrase adorned with a bas-relief of a red purpurine muse against a dark violet background, holding the foot of a red lacquer dog, with the tusks of a wild boar, ears of a hare, wings of a vulture, who seemed to be ravishing and carrying her off, with the inscription in very beautiful and very neat heliotrope runes:

SURGITE MORTUI VENITE AD JUDICIUM DIEI.

The sorrow which the murderer Jörg Michael Günzel of Mauren felt over the loss of his daughter gave rise to illnesses that forced him to remain on his pallet for whole weeks at a time. Before he had even temporarily regained his health, his eyes copper blue, he said:

"Young Frenchman, your coming here has dispelled the happiness in which I delighted. Leave my sight this very instant."

On the organ a trill in an adamantine seventh played with schorl technique.

"And never show your face again in these parts."

I wanted to speak, but he shut my mouth with the lead of his yellowish eyes, and disheartened, driven off, abandoned by one and all, not knowing what would become of me, I started on my way . . .

15

ƒarewell

The next day, at breakfast, I couldn't take my hand away from my right eye because it hurt so much. The count exclaimed in surprise:

"What's wrong? Were you stung by some insect? Did some draft do this to you? We'll stop by the village drugstore before going to the train station. Have you ever been there?"

When I said farewell to the countess I became strangely emotional, all of a sudden I broke down in tears. The children turned from their games to come over and say good-bye. I took one last look at the head of the last wolf, the refreshment stand of the guard, the tower of Mineralogy and Bavarian armoires

(lamellate zeolites, mountain flax actinolites),

the parapet walk, the Torture Chamber Tower

(the last capital execution took place at H— on December 9, 1809:

Johann Kaspar Frisch of Brünsee, for murder, executed by sword;

in that period Napoleon had swallowed up the principality into the kingdom of Bavaria, the Holy Empire no longer existed),

the tower of the Knights' Chamber, the Rotten Tower,

the tower of the library, the church and its bell tower, the bakery and its own, the witch's house . . .

It was the Monday I was leaving, I had to tear myself away, it was high time for me to escape, not only from the castle, not only from Germany . . .

Where, I said, in the train whisking me off, where now, to the other side of Paris?

I have never gone back to H—.

I saw the count again a few years later in Frankfurt; he was a clerk in a bank.

Envoi
The Other Journey

After that, how could I fail to embark for Egypt at the first opportunity?